I0716716

Hope & Fire

L. J. Black

L. J. Black
Hope & Fire
L. J. Black

ACKNOWLEDGEMENTS

The author wishes to thank *Amanda Logue* for her enthusiasm for the author's writing.

For D, the girl I fell in love with

For J, who holds my heart

For all those who still believe in magic

THE WILDLANDS
THE DENT
UMBRA
THE WASTE
MATRAIZE
MATRAIZE
EGRARIA
ATRUS
RESKAL
CHOEQUA
ECRIUM
FALGAR SEA
NAIROCK SEA
EPLYA
ECRIUM
ECRIUM
REBLUINT
NAMORE
APRANA
GAEPIS
PLEASSAU

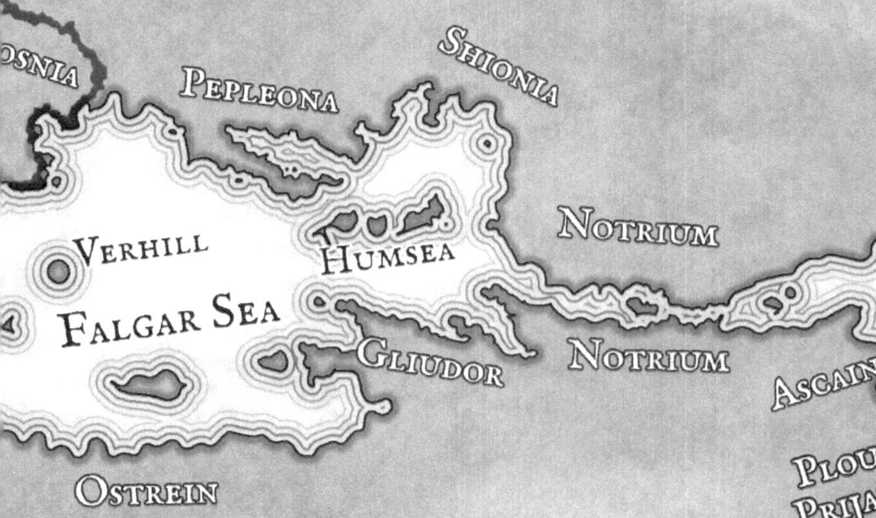

N
XATHEN DESERT
SMAUDAL
OSNIA
PEPLEONA
SHIONIA
NOTRIUM
VERHILL
HUMSEA
FALGAR SEA
GLIUDOR
NOTRIUM
ASCAIN
OSTREIN
PLOU
PRIJAN
THE SOUTHERN WASTE

LECRAIT
LECRAIT

The Waste
Northpass
Aynor Spring
Coreton
Ulheapsa
Avita Spring
Saphlaw
Courtthostur
Egraria
Esaton Cove
Shepport
Port Nalrang
Squall's End
Kurrich
Kynis Beach
Reskal
Ecrium
Falgar Sea
N
Ecrium
Ecrium

SMAUDAL
MOSNIA
FALGAR SEA
VERHILL
PRATERGARDE
REBLUINIA
OSTREIN

Hope & Fire

I am a wicked woman

you cannot handle my power

I live my life beyond the boundaries

of the world's final hour

        ~ Breska Liotson, "Wicked"

Secrets finding their way out of my heart

I hold on to them but they slip through my grip

My fingers feeling the brush of them

As they fly away again

        ~ Breska Liotson, "Broken"

You are my night star

I am the moon in the sky

Apart we shine bright

Together we shine brighter

The darkness recedes from us

        ~ Breska Liotson, "dichotomy"

Prologue

The old witch is dying.

There in the middle of the street, the dust from the road swirls around him in tiny clouds. The crowd pulls away in shock. The knife used to kill him protrudes from his chest in a violent reminder of murder. The murderer did not get far: the patrol officers for Avita Spring already arrested the man responsible. No, not man. The killer is definitely another witch.

At the edge of the dirt road, in front of the line of shops in the center of Avita Spring, Nadia Oswald stands transfixed by the sight of the dying witch. He is old, older than her parents by at least twenty years. She can see his face, his eyes still a bright blue even with the life ebbing out. All those around her, the humans and witches alike, stay at the edges of the street both fascinated and repulsed by the murder. Nadia takes a step forward, a step into that dusty track of road.

The argument leading to the man's death went over her head. One witch fighting with another is not a common occurrence, at least in her experience. Part of her brain recognizes that she has not had much contact with witches, so she cannot know that. She just knows that this argument led to a thrown knife and a dying witch.

"Who is it?" a voice whispers behind her.

"The writer witch," is the reply.

Nadia does not know much about witches or their hierarchy, but even she knows that writer witches are not common. This man's death will be felt.

Unconsciously she has taken several small steps further into the street. She realizes this only when the witch's eyes meet hers. In that moment she realizes they have the same color blue to their eyes. Even as she watches, the color dims a bit.

His hand comes up. Nadia walks forward, stopping only when she gets to the man's side. She kneels in the dirt and takes his hand. Blood begins to stain the pale yellow of her tidy skirt, but she couldn't care less. Something in her couldn't turn away from this dying man.

"What is your name?" he asks. His voice is strained and husky.

"Nadia."

"Are you human?"

Nadia blinks in surprise. To anyone she knows, it is obvious she is human. She is surrounded day in and day out with humans. This witch—this dying man—is the closest to a witch she has been in several years.

"Yes," she answers.

Fear fills his eyes. Nadia feels a shock run through her. She is young enough not to have seen fear like that before. The kind of fear that only comes out when death is at hand. She squeezes his hand tightly, trying to offer the most comfort she can to the dying man with eyes like hers.

His breathing becomes more ragged. He struggles to force out the words. "I'm not done yet—"

Nadia did not get the chance to ask, *With what?* The color goes flat in his eyes and she finds herself holding a corpse.

Try as she might she still cannot let go of the witch's hand. Part of her is horrified by how she continues to hold the dead hand, but somewhere inside of her, she is unable to bring herself to walk away. This man is dead.

Murdered in the street before her eyes. How can she walk away from someone who reached out for her in his last moments, in his last breath?

The air is cold today in their desert town. The wind sends dust everywhere. She is dressed properly in her mother's eyes, with skirts to her ankles and a high collar brushing her chin. She reaches up to brush away a stray hair that has broken loose from her tidy coif. Only when she pulls her hand away does she realize it is covered in blood.

Slowly, gently, she releases her hand from the dead man's. Carefully she places it across his chest and crosses the other hand on top as well. In that moment Nadia realizes she is crying. The glaring knife protruding so invasively from the man's body feels like an offense. This dead witch who reached out to her in his dying moments, she feels he deserves better than to have that knife stuck in him. She reaches out to grab the handle.

"Don't touch it!"

Her hand freezes at the reproof. She looks up to meet the gaze of a patrol officer. He pushes her hand back. He is squatting across the body from her.

Nadia looks at him and takes in the details of her surroundings for the first time in several minutes. Down the street, the patrol officers have subdued the attacker. The crowd has drawn back or been disbursed. And the officer staring at her is middle-aged with black hair and dark brown eyes. His skin is tan as most of his employment are. He wears a crisp uniform in a blue so dark it's almost black. A light dusting of sand, the pervasive sand of Avita, has covered the coat and provided a top layer on his leather boots. His hat held on with a strap sits askew almost jauntily. His expression is not jaunty. His expression scares Nadia. A mixture of fear and pity fills his eyes.

"The knife has a killing spell on it," he explains.

Nadia pulls her hand back to her lap. By now she is simply sitting in the dirt. Her pale-yellow walking suit is taking a beating. She doesn't care.

"Did he say anything to you?" the officer asks.

Absently she glances at his uniform again and sees his surname: Montgomery. She struggles for a moment, trying to remember the first thing the witch asked her. It seems hours ago, or days ago, by now.

"He asked my name."

"Was there—"

"*Nadia!*" a screeching voice interrupts the officer.

Nadia's head whips around at the sound of her

mother's voice—worse, her mother's voice when she is angry. Nadia had been hiding outside the store, hiding from her mother for a reason. Some days her mother's vitriol could not be borne.

"Get up right this instant! Get away from him!"

Without waiting for Nadia to comply, she grips her daughter's arm with brutal force and yanks her to her feet. Nadia's bloody skirts fall back to her ankles. The blood stands out in blinding red against the soft yellows. Even Nadia's dark hair does not compete with the nauseating color.

Her mother, pristine in a plum-velvet suit with ankle-length skirt, proper with a hat perched neatly on her impeccable coif, holds her daughter at arm's length, seemingly to keep the blood away from her person.

Nadia bites the inside of her lip to keep from protesting the hold her mother has on her wrist. She fights hard to keep the tears back. She doesn't want her mother's attention.

Officer Montgomery stands, puffing up to face her mother's tempestuous nature.

"Ma'am, you cannot leave—," he begins—

—"This is a witch's matter, *sir!* This has nothing to do with me or my daughter!" Her mother's rage turns on

Montgomery.   Under the fierce gaze of her mother's anger, he visibly shrinks back and takes several steps away, as if she is somehow on fire.

The scene is ghastly. Nadia is struggling to keep her arm twisted in such a way that her mother doesn't break her wrist. The dead man is on the street between them and Montgomery. The concern on the officer's face when he looks at Nadia is almost more alarming than the previous look he gave her.

"Ma'am—," he tries again—

—"No, *sir!* You can take it up with my husband! He is Edgar Oswald of Oswald and Smythe! You can contact him, sir! We are *leaving!*" She spits the words at him and drags Nadia down the street, through the crowd swiftly parting for them.

The whole way down the street, Nadia endures both the iron-grip of the fiery lady and the constant stream of hissing words— "Nadia! *Really!* What am I going to do with you?! You have no sense! No sense of *decorum!*"— and on and on, right up until Nadia faces the side door of their carriage. The footman opens it for her, and her mother shoves her in.

Nadia sinks into the red leather seats gratefully. It takes all her willpower not to rub her arm where her

mother's fingers had dug in. She is sure there is a bruise forming there.

The carriage starts moving toward home, but her mother has not stopped speaking. She mostly ignores her mother's ongoing lecture on why Nadia is not fit to bear the name Oswald. She can't stand to hear it any longer. Her father isn't like this, but he isn't around much, with his work occupying his time. Her mother hates witches. Any interaction Nadia had with them over the years seemed to evoke a kind of fanatical fervor.

Nadia had a playmate when she was young, a boy named Ethan. He was a local Avita Spring boy, but not an aristocrat. Nadia would slip away almost every day to play with him. When she was six years old, Ethan's grandmother died. He had loved her so much, not just because she was a dear grandparent, but also because she was a witch who enjoyed indulging her grandson. It happened that way sometimes, that a family of humans would have a single witch show up in the genealogy.

When Ethan's grandmother was dying, he wouldn't leave her side for days at a time. He told Nadia later on that his grandmother tried to get him to leave, but he wouldn't go. He held her hand right up until the moment she died. His parents had indulged him, letting him be there with her, even though he was only seven at the time. But Ethan was human and didn't know what happens when a witch dies. As his grandmother's life slipped away, her magic slipped away too, conserved by the world as all energy is conserved. Normally a witch's magic would just fold into the magic of the community, giving all witches nearby a taste of that witch's magic. But if a human is present and in contact with that witch, the magic will be conserved in the human.

Nature abhors a vacuum. The space inside all humans where magic could live is often seen as a vacuum, a void where something else is meant to take root. On that sad evening when Ethan's grandmother died, her magic discovered a void in Ethan and filled it. Ethan walked away from that deathbed with his grandmother's magic in tow. He has been a witch ever since. A week later Nadia's mother forbade her from ever speaking to him again. Nadia never saw him again. He was sent away to a boarding school—a school that taught witchcraft. Her mother would never let her visit. Nadia was even forbidden from writing to him.

Nadia's gaze follows the sidewalk passing their carriage on their way out of the dusty streets of Avita. Ethan comes to mind now as her eyes meet the knowing gaze of many witches along the street. In her heart she already knows the truth, the reason why the dying witch asked if she was human. She already feels the dead witch's magic churning within her. She swallows, her stomach feeling upset now, though not by the blood or the violence. All of her being is in chaos now. As her mother prattles on about the dangers of associating with the wrong people, her heart sinks. The one person she fears the most is sitting across the carriage from her.

"Are you listening to me Nadia?!" her mother's voice cuts into her thoughts. "That's *it!*" Her voice goes up a full octave and Nadia's concerned blue eyes meet her mother's almost-black ones. The sheer force contained behind those eyes is enough to make most people recoil. Sometimes Nadia suspects her mother is some kind of witch in disguise. Or maybe an elemental. A plausible idea with how much she seems to breathe fire all the time.

"What?" Nadia asks, dumbfounded. She really wasn't listening, and she fears she is about to regret it.

Her mother suddenly, completely, calms down.

The hairs go up on the back of Nadia's neck and she swallows again to keep from losing her lunch right there in the carriage.

Her mother smooths her velvet skirt, pats her neat coif, and looks serenely out the window. Every fiber of Nadia's body screams danger.

"I've decided it's time to send you to Fernsby," her mother says. She tries to do it almost regally, but the effect is lost with the evil glint in her eye.

Nadia takes back all her assessments from a moment ago. Her mother is a demon, no doubt about it. Fernsby School for Girls is a boarding school specializing in shaping young ladies of character. The school is located in Coreton, over two hundred miles away, precariously perched on the western edge of the northern plateau. And not one stitch of magic is taught in the place.

"Mother!"

Her mother waves one pointed finger at her. "Not another word," she says calmly. "You are going and that's final."

Nadia's heart falls. She goes back to looking out the window. There is no arguing with her mother when she is like this. She would try to talk her father into letting her stay, but he rarely disagrees with her mother where Nadia is concerned. It is a lost battle to begin with.

She swallows, a dryness settling into her throat that has nothing to do with the weather. Spring is nearly over and summer is almost here. But Fernsby is year-round, by all accounts. She could start tomorrow and not be home for a year—or years.

At the moment the prospect of rarely seeing her mother tantalizes her. But at only ten years old she faces several lengthy years at an academy where magic is forbidden. The feisty spark inside her knows this will not do to be exiled. She will find a way to beat this.

One

Aidan Montgomery lifts his hand and shields his eyes from the sun. He stands far out in the middle of the plateau. The town is somewhere in the distance behind him, but he doesn't know exactly where.

"Where are we?" John Blestone asks.

Aidan looks up at the sun to make a show of knowing where they are. He doesn't know. That is the point of the exercise though. Not knowing and finding.

"Which way do we go?"

"I don't know," Aidan answers. "You're the seer. You tell me."

John rolls his eyes. He sets his jaw and concentrates. Aidan waits. He knows John is not as proficient as their teacher. And Aidan is not a seer. He struggles with the process.

"Southeast."

Aidan nods.

"You still got nothing?" John asks.

Not wanting to admit his failure, Aidan doesn't say a word.

"Aidan, you're going to have to learn eventually."

He swallows and says, "I know. But not right now."

"*When?* It's been four years."

"I know," he whispers, pulling his goggles back over his eyes. He wraps his turban about his chin and covers his nose and mouth. John follows Aidan's gaze and mirrors his action. In the distance a dust storm is kicking up and will likely overtake them before they make it back to town. With a glance over his shoulder and an adjustment of his sleeves, Aidan heads off toward the southeast. He can practically hear John roll his eyes as he follows.

Silence envelopes them. Only the sound of their boots crunching the gravel disturbs the air. The sun behind them beats down ferociously. Aidan's tan skin is covered protectively to the wrists and ankles, not just from the sun but the unforgiving cold. Thin strips poke between the folds of fabric here and there, just barely allowing him to feel the extreme chill in the air.   They keep moving, plodding forward to stay warm.

Somewhere in the distance the Spike, a training tool of unknown form detectable only through magic and power, is hidden in the sands and cliffs of the desert. Each witch is partnered with another of differing capabilities and sent on this trek at different points in their schooling. John is a seer, the lowest and most common form of witch. Aidan is an anchor, though few even in his school are aware. A Gag casting is placed around him, working on all witches he meets to never speak of his ability. Only those who already know or who learn it from Aidan himself can speak of it and only when he lifts the spell. This is why John is careful in his word choice when speaking to Aidan. This is why John never tells Aidan he must learn sometime to be an *anchor.* John simply cannot speak the words.

But what does it even mean to be an anchor? Aidan wonders as they walk across the open desert plane. The dust slowly kicks up around them and he adjusts the scarf covering his mouth and nose. No matter how many times he asks his instructors, older witches—anyone really—they don't know. His instructors tell him he will find his own path as all anchors have done before him. But it doesn't feel right to him. Anchors are stable, solid people whose lives are far more predictable than Aidan's. Maybe it is just the time they live in and the period of unrest. He doesn't know.

Aidan's right foot comes down and an internal bell clangs silently in his heart, the shockwave radiating out from his toes. He stops in his tracks.

John has taken two steps before he turns back, confused. "What is it?" John asks.

"It's under here," Aidan says certainly, looking at the ground. They have not been walking that long and he is surprised at where they are standing.

Kneeling down, his knees scraping the sand-gravel mixture, Aidan puts his bare hands on the unforgiving ground. Their planet suffered long ago the strike of a passing planetoid, a passing that nearly destroyed the early world. This desert plateau is one of the many remnants of that chaotic past. Aidan can almost feel the echoes of that explosion within them.

"I can't see anything," John says. He is kneeling next to Aidan, trying to see through the ground.

"I am sure it is below us," Aidan insists.

John sighs. "Should we try the casting?" His voice is weary. As a seer, castings are a tier above him and therefore difficult to do. Aidan is two tiers above casting, so they present little challenge. And he has always been comfortable doing them and that makes all the difference.

Aidan holds out his left hand and John obligingly takes it. They have been partners for many years now and this has become second nature to them. This particular casting, designed to reveal the Spike wherever it may be, never troubles them when they work it together.

There are no words, there is only a blending of power. Power, that extension of magic all witches possess, flexes in response to the witch's particular affiliation and any lower affiliation but no higher. Only when working together are they able to overcome their bounds.

Beneath their hands the ground opens up for a moment, becomes transparent though never impermeable. The illusion is unnerving. Though they know they are perfectly safe, they both feel as if they are floating in midair waiting to fall. But the Spike is visible. Below the ground, below them, several feet down in fact.

Through their casting bond, Aidan feels John's surprise. The Spike is well-buried, no doubt about that, but he was unable to detect it. With his free hand John reaches down to grasp the object, today what looks like a small lute constructed of reedwood. John's hand passes right through it.

"I can't get it," he says, shock registering in his voice.

Aidan reaches down and closes his fingers around the wooden object. It comes to the surface with no resistance. Dumbfounded Aiden sits staring at the lute. He has never been able to do anything John *couldn't* do, though by definition he should be able to do many things John couldn't.

"Maybe that's why they sent us out today," John says.

"Maybe," Aidan answers, thinking of all the frustration he's felt the past four years. A moment or so passes before he snaps himself back to the present. "We should head back."

While they have been sitting, the dust storm has begun to kick up. Aidan tucks the Spike in his jacket pocket and they head back toward town.

"Ethan is never going to believe this," John remarks.

"Why would Ethan care?" Aidan asks.

"He bet me we'd come back empty-handed." He glances at Aidan. "He'll have to do my chores this week."

Aidan laughs. "A good bet then."

They push forward into the dust.

Two

"We should get going."

Nadia adjusts her hat and her skirt. She takes the hand offered to her and mounts the horse. These are not the average horses seen pulling plows only a few miles over. These are the tough giant beasts normally running wild in the dunes of the lower deserts. Nadia feels small and precarious perched on the mare's tall back. At age thirteen she is still a small person.

The journey ahead of her is a long one. Roads too treacherous for carriages face them as they cross the plateau. Her third year at Fernsby awaits her return. Unexpected friends would meet her there again, and she looked forward to their reunion. Her two week break with her family only served to put her under her mother's judgmental gaze again. How she kept her writer witch powers from her mother during the past two weeks, she wasn't sure. Even with a dearth of magical practice, the girls at Fernsby have made it a home for her.

"Are you ready?"

Nadia checks her seat, makes sure her knee is secure in the side-saddle. She doesn't need to fall off the great beast before they even leave town. And she would switch to sitting astride when they leave the edges of town.

"Ready, Mr. Kaye," she says, nodding to the man. He is her father's assistant and has ridden with her on every journey up north to school. This is the last day of this journey, the second night they stopped for an evening. The inn in Ulheapsa has become familiar to her in the years since she started at Fernsby. The staff recognizes them as they arrive. Even now Mrs. Keys walks up to the side of her horse and hands up a small cloth parcel.

"For the journey, Miss Oswald. Some of your favorites."

Nadia smiles knowing they are small lemon cakes. The lemon comes from the two trees grown in the inn's courtyard and drawn on the sign hanging near her head.

She thanks Mrs. Keys and tucks the parcel into the pocket of her skirt for later.

"Be safe, Miss Oswald. I hope we'll see you on the return journey," Mrs. Keys says.

Nadia reaches down and squeezes Mrs. Keys hand, saying, "No doubt you will."

She straightens up, brings her veil down over her face and tugs her brim forward a bit to block the sun, and nods at Kaye to signal she's ready. He nods back and begins a slow trot away from the inn. Nadia follows, guiding her horse expertly. After a few moments she looks over her shoulder at Mrs. Keys and waves. Then they are on their way, heading out of Ulheapsa, this small town in the northern plateau.

About an hour outside of town, Nadia swings her leg over the saddle and spurs her horse forward to draw even with Kaye. A length of turban fabric covers his mouth to protect himself from the dust of the desert. Without her face veil or the brim of her hat, the oppressive desert heat would wear her out almost immediately. Fortunately, this road they travel is not only a familiar one, but a well-used one, the thunk of thick stone beneath horse hooves a comforting sound.

By midday they would reach their resting point, a

small inn at the midway point between Ulheapsa and Coreton. A no-name non-town, the inn is the only thing for miles around it, made possibly only by a lone well providing the building with water. Too measly a supply for a large number of inhabitants, only the proprietor and their family live at the inn. They would not stay overnight there, but only for a few hours to wait out the hottest part of the day.

"Are you ready to be back?" Kaye asks.

"Yes," Nadia answers almost immediately. "I miss my friends, but I think you know that."

Though she can't see his smile under the face covering, she knows he is smiling at her from his eyes. "I imagine Elise will be happy you're back."

Nadia smiles immediately thinking of her best friend. Elise comes from Umbra, the country to the north across the Waste, the great desert division. More than just being from Umbra, her family are aristocrats. Elise's grandmother was the Queen's sister, daughter of the former King. While Elise carries the title of Princess and certainly could use it if she wanted to, she says it's pointless given that between all her cousins, aunts, and uncles she's eleventh in line for the throne. Her royal ties have been a boon for Nadia. While Elise is not a witch and few in her family are, she was able to procure witch reading materials for Nadia over the years. Without Elise's help, Nadia would have no control over her power.

"Yes, she'll be back from Umbra next week."

"Those new flying ships will certainly help with her travel," Kaye remarks.

"Would you ride in one of them?" Nadia asks.

"They've only been around a few years, but it must be interesting." He looks at her and says, "Would you? Or would you prefer to fly like regular witches?"

Nadia laughs. "If I ever learn that," she says.

"Does it bother you that you're at such a disadvantage?"

Nadia pauses before answering. Kaye always speaks to her as if she is an adult, which is more than her parents do. So sometimes it catches her off guard that he asks her opinion.

"I'm not sure I would say it bothers me that I'm at a disadvantage exactly," she says slowly. "It bothers me more that my own family wouldn't accept me."

"Your mother more than your father," Kaye remarks.

"You think my father is more accepting?"

Kaye shrugs. "Perhaps I am biased," he says. "But you know my beliefs and I think you know I would not work for your father if I thought he was truly prejudiced."

Nadia's glance falls on the tiny pin Kaye wears on his jacket. He never wears it around her parents, but he wears it around Nadia to show his support for her. The tiny pin consists of a pair of crescent moons with a leaf embedded behind it: the symbol of the Fellowship of Allkind. The Fellowship accepts all people—human, witch, and even elementals. That kind of open-minded acceptance was not a part of Nadia's childhood.

They fall into silence for a while, only the horse hooves breaking it with their rhythmic clop on the road. The scenery around them opens up a bit as they get further away from Ulheapsa. The town sits in the shadow of the last hills before the plateau flattens out heading to cliffs. From here almost to their last steps before Coreton, the geography would continue in a flat desert, sand blowing occasionally around them and little vegetation to break up the monotony.

Coreton sits almost on the precipice of the cliffs, overlooking the Waste and the Dent, that remnant of the near meteor impact in their archaic past that left a deep and unforgettable scar on their planet. North of the divide sits Umbra, under that glimmering witch shield laid down at the founding of the nation. Sometimes Nadia looks across the Dent in the direction of the shield and wonders what it must be like living in such an accepting country that they trust their safety to the charge of witches.

About two hours had passed when Kaye suddenly grabs the reins of Nadia's horse and brings both beasts to a halt. Smart enough not to protest, especially here in the middle of the desert, she looks at Kaye and then follows his gaze.

For a moment she can't figure out what Kaye is looking at, then in a flash of movement she sees them. The land slopes upwards slightly to a rise probably half a mile away. There at the peak a pair of creatures lock in battle with each other. The flashes of movement and glimmer of light tickle Nadia's senses now that she's focused on them. She can feel the power of them, a much greater and more primitive power than the witch power she carries inside her.

"Are they elementals?" Kaye whispers. As a human, he would not have the delicate sensibilities to distinguish between the various creatures.

"No," Nadia whispers back. "They are spirits. I'm not sure what kind." She has not read enough about spirits to be able to identify them.

"Do you think we can pass them safely?" Kaye asks.

Nadia pauses. "I think so, but we must be careful."

Kaye lets go the reins and both urge their horses forward slowly. Nadia watches surreptitiously as the horses creep past. The spirits seem locked in what they are doing, unaware or uninterested in the corporeal beings passing them. Before too long she and Kaye have passed them by and they round a bend in the road, a slight rise in the landscape putting the spirits out of sight.

"What kind do you think they were?" Kaye asks after they had been traveling a few minutes.

Nadia smiles to herself. "Sand probably."

She glances at Kaye in time to see him roll his eyes. "Are you this serious about your studies?" he asks dryly.

"Only math."

With that they lapse into silence for another hour.

Three

The edges of town seemingly appear out of nowhere, the first few buildings in this desert oasis give way in the sand. Courtthostur is a small town, packed in around a series of natural springs near the center of it. It's mid-southern location in the kingdom means some of the scraggly plants of the north give way to palms and ferns more closely resembling those that live along the plateau coast. There the tall buttresses of rock enrobed in green and surrounded by deep water host millions of citizens in large metropolises. Courtthostur is home to maybe ten thousand people, smaller than the neighboring oasis of Saphlaw, which hosts half again as many people.

Small farms circle the springs at the center of town,

followed by sections of residential districts and various shops and cafes, especially on the western side that faces Saphlaw. Since they're approaching from the east, they head down a sandy alley between rows of towering houses. The adobe garden sidewalls conceal the sandy desert courtyards common in Courtthostur, melding into the walls of two- and three-story houses with thick, insulating walls. Ice fans keep most houses cool in Courtthostur, which helped houses grow from the squat single-story buildings more common in the inner rings to the taller luxurious houses at the edges of town.

At the end of the alley, Aidan and John turn right and head up the outer lane. Courtthostur Academy sits on the northern side of town, occupying a series of converted houses. They walk through neighborhoods closer and closer to the center springs, passing the farms at the center of town. Finally, they round the last corner to the school buildings and enter the arched gate in the outer walls. Students still scatter around the outer courtyard, a tight knit group of girls lounging under a grove of palms, a few of the younger boys tossing rocks into the fountain and subsequently getting yelled at by one of the professors.

"Hey!" a voice calls from the doorway to the main

building.

"Hey, Ethan," Aidan says.

John chuckles.

"What?" Ethan asks.

John just holds up the Spike.

"What?!" Ethan says again. He looks at Aidan incredulously and back at John. "You got it?!"

"Yes," John answers, "and you better live up to your bet."

By now half the courtyard is staring at them. Most have known Aidan's struggle with his anchor power, even if they are not aware it is anchor power he struggles with. An odd silence falls over the gathered students as their writer witch professor comes out of the main building accompanied by the dean of the witch school. The pair approach them, the laughter and ridiculousness fading though John is clearly having a hard time keeping a straight face.

Aidan straightens up as the two come nearer. Professor Effie Goliyant, the resident writer witch and general spell expert, stands a head taller than the dean. Her skin, the color of ochre highlighted with a golden glow, offsets the bright hazel of her eyes and complements the few dark strands of hair peeking out from under her white veil. The head covering so common in the deserts matches her white academic's robe worn over her more modern dove grey walking suit. How she keeps that ensemble from getting any dust on it has to be a magical quest all on its own.

She smiles at Aidan, but the dean looks stern as usual. The formidable caster witch is shorter than Aidan himself, but he still intimidates with just his presence. A native of Port Nalrang, the metropolis on the southern coastlines, Dean Jaran Watters once told Aidan that he misses the bustling streets and the deep waters of his home.

"So, Mr. Montgomery," the Dean says, "I see you found it."

"Yes, Dean Watters."

The Dean holds out his hand and John offers him the Spike. Dean Watters inspects it with interest and says, "Delicate work, Effie."

Aidan's gaze shifts to Professor Goliyant.

"Yes, I wrote the script," she confirms with a slight smile. "A tidy piece of work."

"Indeed," Dean Watters says. He hands the Spike to Aidan saying, "Yours I believe. Don't slip backward now, Mr. Montgomery. I know you struggle with your place, but we all do that. It's important to make the most of where we belong."

Aidan takes the Spike and nods. Dean Watters gives John and Ethan a knowing look and then turns to head back in the building. Professor Goliyant looks amused as she follows.

There is a pause. Then John says to Ethan, "So you're doing my chores, right?"

Ethan rolls his eyes, sighs, and walks away. John follows him.

Aidan smiles at the Spike for a moment before heading after his partner and friend.

Four

At some point Nadia realizes the distant spot in the flat landscape is the inn at the halfway point between Ulheapsa and Coreton. As they inch forward the building seems to grow slowly on the horizon before suddenly, almost all at once, leaping to full size only a few feet from them.

The inn has seen better days, or perhaps it's just the persistent layer of dirt and dust on everything that makes it seem unkempt. Adobe bricks constructed in the old style show crumbling around the edges, with the mortar between them breaking apart in some spots. The sandy color, likely from the sand the bricks were constructed of, runs right into the surrounding sands, washing everything into a single layer of tawny brown. Large windows flanked by heavy-looking wooden shutters likely came in from Ulheapsa or even further away as trees do not grow in the Northern Plateau. Windows frame out two stories in the center part of the building, but to either side a single floor reaches out. There are rooms available for rent on either side of the central space, but seldom do any travelers stay the night here. Within a concealed courtyard, a likely-expensive glass greenhouse pokes out, its spires jutting above the walls. The greenhouse is notably newer than the surrounding building.

A woman steps into the open double doors at the center of the building, shielding her eyes in the steadily brightening noonday sun. From here Nadia can see two other horses tied to a post under a shelter with a water trough. They are not the first visitors of the day and will likely not be the last.

Kaye dismounts and holds the reins steady while Nadia follows suit. The woman takes the bridles and greets them warmly.

"How are you Mrs. Palmer?"

"Doing well, and yourself Miss Oswald?" she asks.

"Parched I'm afraid."

Mrs. Palmer smiles widely. "Well go inside. Ask my wife to get you some lemonade."

"Thank you. I'd be grateful."

Kaye holds the door for Nadia as they walk into the common area of the inn. A table to the left up against a wall hosts the two others resting here. They nod in Nadia and Kaye's direction, who return the silent greeting. Both have their heads still covered, but their face scarves are lowered for the sake of drinking. Behind the bar Mrs. Palmer's wife Mrs. Mueller smiles in greeting and comes around the counter to embrace Nadia. The warmth of Mrs. Mueller's caster witch power presses comfortably up against Nadia's writer witch strength.

"How are you doing, dear?" she asks familiarly.

"Tired and hot, but well otherwise," Nadia answers. It is not a secret Nadia is a witch. Her mother does not know, and certainly no one around her mother dares tell her because of the backlash they would receive. But Nadia herself is not able to hide it out in public. Most humans would not pick up on the subtle writer witch power, but every witch, elemental, and spirit would know immediately. Whether it's wise she cannot hide it or not, she doesn't know. The power's previous owner was murdered after all.

"Let me get you a cold drink," Mrs. Mueller answers as she greets Kaye with a nod of the head and a smile.

She gestures to a table at the right side of the room and returns behind the bar to get them each a drink.

Nadia and Kaye sit opposite each other, Nadia lifting her face veil and Kaye lowering his face wrap for now. She glances around at the half dozen tables and wonders if there ever is a time when all of them are occupied. Probably a rare occasion at this out-of-the-way stopping point.

Mrs. Mueller sets a couple of glasses on the table then pours lemonade from an ice-cold pitcher in her hand. The beverage is so cold that condensation is dripping down the sides of the pitcher. Mrs. Mueller uses her caster power frequently to keep beverages cold in the desert climate. Nadia drinks from the glass and smiles at the tart-sweet juice.

"Did these come from Ulheapsa?"

"Of course. Where all our lemons come from."

Mrs. Mueller sits down with them. "So, tell me the news. How are things back home?"

Nadia sets her glass down. Before leaving Avita Spring for Coreton, Nadia would not have considered her small hometown as a bustling center of activity. Her years of traveling through these out-of-the-way hamlets told her differently. The witchwire sends messages and news to the far reaches of the kingdom, and indeed the rest of the world. But smaller stories and gossip don't make it in the news. That's what Mrs. Mueller wants to talk about.

About fifteen minutes pass of Nadia gossiping with Mrs. Mueller when Mrs. Palmer comes back in and smiles at them. "How are we doing now?" she asks.

"Better," Nadia answers.

"Anything interesting to report?"

Kaye looks sidelong at Mrs. Palmer and says, "There were two spirits in a tangle about an hour east of here."

Mrs. Palmer's eyebrows go up in response to this news. She exchanges a glance with her wife. "They are restless these days," she comments.

"Have you had any pass through recently?" Nadia asks. As she has known for years, the inn does not ward against spirits out here. There would be no point. The open plateau is their domain. Elise has told her the Waste is the same way: a wild desert domain where spirits tend to roam. Conversely, the towns of Coreton and Northpass guard against them.

"About a month ago," Mrs. Mueller answers. "They went through the greenhouses and caused everything to bloom early."

Involuntarily, Nadia smiles. The idea of spirits going through the greenhouse and all the plants blooming at once seemed like a piece of beautiful magic.

Mrs. Palmer gives Nadia a look. "Oh, sure it's funny now. But you didn't have to can a year's worth of produce in the space of a week."

Nadia burst out laughing as did Mrs. Mueller.

"My wife neglects to tell you that they were the best vegetables we've ever had come out of the greenhouses," Mrs. Mueller says.

Mrs. Palmer rolls her eyes and walks away. Mrs. Mueller taps the table and follows her saying, "I'll get you both something to eat."

After a moment, Kaye says, "I wonder why the spirits are so restless."

"I don't know," Nadia answers, "but it's usually a portent of something."

"All the more reason to get you to a place you can actually cultivate your talent."

She doesn't answer, just studies her glass of lemonade sweating in the desert heat. She pulls the cuff of her sleeves back, letting her wrists cool off a bit. It's a small act of defiance she would not get away with if her mother were around. She runs a finger through the condensation and applies it to her bare wrists, reveling in the cooling it gives. The desert may be dry and therefore not overbearing in its heat, but it is still hot.

"What do you think I should do?" Nadia asks Kaye. She genuinely respects and wants his opinion. Of all the people in her life, perhaps three know the full extent of her circumstances and Kaye is one of them.

He finishes a long drink of lemonade and refills the glass before answering. "You need a place to practice your craft outside of your mother's sight," he starts. "That is the crux of the problem. I do not believe you can do so if you move home." Nadia nods in agreement. "So we must find a way to get you into a college or university that offers it, not as its first subject but as an option."

Nadia mulls this over in silence, thinking that she is at least four years from that possibility. It's true that Elise helped provide her materials in the past few years, but by any metric she was almost hopelessly behind in the practice of her writer witch abilities. How could she hope to catch up enough to be useful in four years?

"That is a long time away," she says softly, staring at the table.

"Mmm," Kaye murmurs in agreement. "I wonder . .

.” He trails off and when she looks at him his eyes are fixed out the window over the door where the vista shows a dust storm has started rolling through.

Almost in unison Nadia and Kaye, as well as the two gentlemen at the other table, rise and head for the front wall windows to peer at the sudden storm. A lone figure outside comes to the door and opens and shuts it with the brisk efficiency of one who has dealt with dust storms before. The stranger steps away from the door and Mrs. Palmer approaches him. He takes off his hat and lowers the scarf to reveal a face not older than mid-thirties but cracked with deep wrinkles as if he is much older. The clear blue eyes briefly glance in her direction. Immediately Nadia knows he's not human.

"Can I help you?" Mrs. Palmer asks cordially.

"Just something to drink, thank you," the man answers. His voice is gravely and no wonder with the dust kicking up out there. Mrs. Palmer nods and returns to the bar passing Mrs. Mueller who is holding a glass of lemonade.

"Is this alright?" she asks.

The man smiles, a gesture which clearly is well-meant but does little more than crack the gruff face with the expression. The bristly mustache and beard, no doubt uncomfortable in the weather as it is, twitch as he lifts the glass to take a deep drink. Nadia studies the motion, studies the way the condensation on the glass moves atypically toward his skin and not with gravity. By the time he lowers the now-empty glass, the condensation has lined his bare hand completely.

One glance at Kaye and Mrs. Mueller and Nadia knows neither of them missed it either. The man before them is either an extremely powerful water caster or he is flat out an elemental.

Mrs. Mueller takes the empty glass back as the man chokes out a gruff "Thank you."

"Will you need to stay the night?" she asks.

"It depends on how long the storm persists," he answers. "I dislike traveling in the dust."

"Don't we all," Kaye mutters, guiding Nadia back to their seats.

Mrs. Mueller entreats the man to take a seat and he does at the table adjacent to Nadia and Kaye. The other men have returned to their table, now seemingly resigned to staying longer as the weather has taken a turn.

"What were you saying before?" Nadia asks.

Kaye snaps out of his reverie and his stare at the stranger, looks back at Nadia. "I was only thinking we might get you on an internship at one of the schools that teaches the craft."

The idea blossoms in Nadia's mind. The possibilities immediately fall open from it. "You mean one with a writer at it," she says.

Kaye nods slowly. "I don't have the authority to pull such strings, but maybe your dean can look into it."

Nadia's eyebrows quirk and she tilts her head in thought going over how that conversation might go. As her school goes, the Dean is probably the most open to the idea of teaching the craft, though she is barred from doing so at the school. The one witch on staff, Ms. Goldrich who teaches mathematics, is a proficient caster but is disallowed from teaching Nadia. Only a handful of witch students attend the school, all of them from wealthy influential families perfectly capable of getting them private study under a high-ranking, prominent, or powerful witch of their choice. All except Nadia whose family frowns upon it.

The feeling of ruefulness deep in her chest curls her lip in a way her mother would have scolded. As it is her eyes look up to see the stranger studying her. She quelches her feelings immediately.

"You are untrained," he remarks.

Nadia's eyes narrow. There is nothing so unsafe as being an untrained, rare-power witch in the presence of a lower-ranking one. Especially a stranger whose intentions she doesn't know. Kaye immediately straightens and sets a hand on the table. A long menacing dagger sits under the hand.

The stranger's eyes dart to the knife and back to Nadia, a sense of understanding dawning in them. "You are mistaken, I'm not interested in your power," he says. "I have more than I need."

By way of explanation, he flicks a finger at the glasses on their table and the condensation on them as well as the water soaked into the table responds immediately to fly across the room and rest in a sphere before the directing finger.

Nadia stares at the easy manipulation of water and re-examines her perceptions of the man. Certainty eclipses doubt. "An elemental," she says softly.

The man tips his head down in acknowledgement. His too-young face of leathered skin suddenly makes sense. The dryness of the desert must be hell to pass through if you are a water elemental.

"Why are you way out here?" she asks, aware the question might be impertinent.

The mustache twitches. "I am passing through like you. To Umbra eventually."

Umbra, the closest large water source, home to the great polar cap.

"Is the polar cap your destination?" Kaye asks cordially.

The elemental smiles in amusement. "The cap, yes, but I am headed for Arcta."

"Oh!" Nadia says involuntarily. Arcta is the capital of Umbra and incidentally also Elise's home, her family being part of the royal family.

"You know it?" the elemental asks, surprised.

"Not exactly," Nadia admits. "A friend is from there."

"Ah," he says. "Then you should visit. And look me up when you come."

"What is your name?"

His faint smile vanishes completely replaced by a rueful expression. "I had one once, but they call me Hydris now."

"What *was* your name?" Nadia pursues. The fact that he has a call name tells her he wasn't born a water elemental but, like Nadia, became one.

"Adriel Porter," he answers with another of those

smiles, "but you would only find me as Hydris."

Nadia nods, memorizing the name for later. Not all witches scribble their thoughts down, but most writer witches do. Nadia doesn't yet keep a notebook for her work.

"Do you know who you inherited the writer witch power from?" Hydris asks.

Nadia nodded. "He was the writer witch in my hometown. The only one in Avita Spring I believe." She did not explain the exact circumstances of her inheritance or her family's ignorance of it. She learned the hard way that telling people you witnessed a murder of a prominent witch and held his hand when he was dying was an easy way to make them look at you as if you yourself were a ghost.

Hydris looks at her curiously but does not ask any further questions. Perhaps he feels it would be impolite to do so.

Mrs. Mueller chooses that moment to approach the table and let them know their usual suite is ready for a respite if they choose. Kaye thanks her kindly and together with Nadia they get up from the table.

"It was a pleasure to meet you, Mr. Porter," Nadia says, choosing to use his older name.

A smile crosses the elemental's face, a genuine deep smile that brings out a glimmer in his eyes. "And you as well," he says. "What was your name?"

Kaye stiffens. Nadia's family name conjures too many anti-witch sentiments. Her mother's, and by association her father's, campaigns against the increasing presence of witches in all walks of life are too widely known.

Nadia swallows and says, "Nadia Oswald."

Hydris's eyebrows go up slightly. He nods as if her predicament suddenly makes sense to him. "I hope you do look me up in Arcta when you visit." He extends his hand to her.

Kaye relaxes next to her. Nadia takes the proffered hand. "I'll be sure to," she promises.

The touch of Hydris's power in her palm stays with her up the staircase, as they turn onto the second flight of stairs, and she hears him asking Mrs. Palmer if he can do some work in their greenhouse for them. She doesn't hear the answer, but several minutes later in the parlor of their suite, Nadia watches from the window as the water elemental spins careful ribbons of precious liquid from the trough. The ribbons weave in an intricate dance through the parched air and settle in each of the long planters.

A shiver runs up Nadia's spine.

For just a moment she can see a flicker of fire and water and a machine so great she cannot imagine its purpose. She can feel the heat of the fire on her face. Several people stand near her, but she cannot turn her head to see them, her gaze fixed on that broad wall of metal, that huge machine. The heat of the nearest body presses on her right side, her body feeling the presence of power and recognizing it there. She turns her head—

And the inn snaps into view around her.

Below in the courtyard Hydris still moves bands of water back and forth.

Across the room Kaye has taken a seat and sits dozing with his hat over his eyes.

Only a few moments have passed. Nadia feels as if an age has come between her and the version of herself that came up the stairs. For a moment Hydris pauses, sensing her eyes on him, and turns to look up at the window.

They lock eyes and then he goes back to moving water around under the supervision of Mrs. Palmer.

Five

Aidan rounds the corner of the main hallway and walks up to the doorway of Effie Goliyant's office. The adobe walls were painted and sealed with a taupe paint that was refreshed just earlier this year. Aidan stares at that paint, waiting for Professor Goliyant to call him in. He doesn't have to wait long.

"Aidan," she calls softly. Her voice still carries through the wall and he pushes through the door. On the other side he finds Effie Goliyant seated behind a large metal desk scattered with parchment and slate tablets and books and scrolls and even thick stone volumes that must weigh a ton: all trappings of her witch side. She pushes back from her desk, her metal stool scraping the floor obnoxiously. A flick of a hand and the dinky wooden stool next to him clears its contents obligingly. "Have a seat Mr. Montgomery." Another flick of her hand and her desk accouterments move over enough that she doesn't have to peer around stacks to see him.

He sits on the precarious old wooden stool, a material not seen much around Courtthostur.

"How are things going?"

Aidan shrugs. She always starts these meetings with this question, and he never has a good answer. Never seems to have *any* answer. It's been weeks since he found the Spike and the odd little object sits on his desk in his study to remind him that he is able to do things. Not much has happened since then though.

"I don't know," he says honestly.

"No progress, even incrementally?" she asks.

Aidan slouches in his seat and stares out the window overlooking the far side of town and the vast emptiness of the plateau. "No, not really."

Professor Goliyant sits back until she is leaning on the wall behind her. Her head is framed by the soft orange-yellow light of late afternoon turning to sunset.

"I think I have an idea that may help you," she says.

Aidan's eyes flick back to her immediately.

"You are aware we are hosting the quarterly forum

next month," she says.

He nods though he had forgotten the meeting is next month. Too deep in the day-to-day grit of his student life, he had forgotten what time of the year it was.

"We will be hosting all classifications of witches from all over the world," she continues. "Admittedly it is the smallest meeting of the year, so we won't have everyone I would want here." A brief look of annoyance flits across her face with that statement. "However, I think we can use it as a pretense to invite an anchor witch here."

Aidan's interest is piqued. He doesn't know of any anchor witches though he knows there are a few, maybe a handful total, in the whole world. "Would any be able to come?" he asks, hiding his enthusiasm behind a bland expression. "And how much would I be able to learn in only a week?"

Effie's face twists as she calculates. "Admittedly, not much," she says, "but the point is to create a dialogue between you." She leans forward again and holds up a hand. "Now I know there are maybe five or six anchors, and like you they tend to stay hidden. The only one I know of presents himself as an advanced caster witch."

Aidan nods, taking in that information. "Am I just

going to be hiding myself my whole life too?" he says out loud without meaning to.

Her eyes study him with sympathy. "I know it's difficult," she says. "But there are so few anchors. You can break the spell anytime," she reminds him. He has known this since she laid the binding around him. His power supersedes hers, and thus she could not spell him directly, just spell around him. If he chose to tell someone what he is, the spell would not be able to stop him. John was the first person he used this privilege on. The trust had proved to be well-placed.

"I know," he says. "But you are right."

"I don't have to be right forever," she answers.

They lapse into silence, each deep in their own thoughts.

Then she leans forward, her elbows on the desk and asks, "Should I invite the anchor?"

Startled Aidan looks up at her. "Yes," he says, slightly confused because he thought she had already decided.

"It is and always will be your decision," she says. "Your power, your choice."

Another phrase she repeats frequently.

"I admit I feel strongly you should master it, but I do

not require it of you," she says. "You can choose to be a simple caster witch your whole life."

Aidan shrugs. "It's . . . not that," he says slowly. Not for the first time he struggles to find the right words. This time, for the first time maybe, he feels he should try.

Effie sits patiently watching him.

"It's odd." Immediately he hates the words. "I just don't feel like . . . an anchor. Or that I'm supposed to be an anchor." He shakes his head. "I know I'm supposed to be one, but I don't feel like I'm . . . stable enough."

"You don't feel immovable, as an anchor should be," Professor Goliyant says.

"Yes."

Effie's mouth twitches as if she is containing a smile. "First, you should give yourself a break. You are still young, you're not even fifteen yet?" she asks.

"Yes, I'll be fifteen next month."

"Exactly. To be an anchor is to know who you are well enough to move or hold the world." She flicks her hand almost dismissively as she adds, "Of course I cannot speak to this directly. But it is the same as I felt when I was younger. I struggled to read and write as a child."

Aidan blinks in surprise. A writer witch who couldn't read and write comfortably seemed impossible.

"It's true," she says, confirming his incredulity. "I could have been a caster or even a seer if that's what it came to. But I overcame the obstacles in front of me. I found a way to work through it and learn to write."

Aidan shakes his head. *"How?"*

A small smile crosses Effie's face. "I started with oral traditional spells, the spells woven into stories." She shrugs. "If the usual path doesn't work, make another way."

Aidan mulishly thinks this over. He doesn't think his problems are quite the same as not being good at reading and writing. The comparison does not sit well with him.

"Is your uncle coming to visit?"

Professor Goliyant changes the subject, clearly ready to move on.

"Yes," Aidan answers, his mind only half on the conversation.

A half hour later he leaves her office completely unable to recall their conversation past that point. His mind fixates on both the idea of a writer witch with reading and writing difficulties and the future meeting with the anchor.

His stomach growls and Aidan turns a corner, heading down the stairs for lunch.

Six

Every Sammday, the fourth day of the school week, during their free hour in the afternoon, Nadia and Elise walk into Coreton and have tea together at a quiet tea shop. The shop changes, as there are a few to choose from in Coreton, but they always find a quiet corner away from people at which they can spend the time catching up. Today their break is a bit longer, so they make the walk across town to Sheffield's Tea Room at the far end of Arrowwood Alley, so named because of the cluster of arrowwood trees growing at the near end of it.

They take the turn under the shade of those trees, fed by a magically created spring in the center of them, and head down the narrow alleyway from the founding of the town. There the adobe brick buildings get closer together, their facades more worn down with time. Only an occasional shrub perched on a high porch or roof as is customary provides momentary shade. The girls share a white lace parasol given to Elise for her birthday last year. The afternoon heat bears down on them.

Around the last bend of the alley, through a narrow passage between some much older houses, they come to the little courtyard where Sheffield's doors wait open on the right. To the left across the terracotta tiles, about fifteen feet away in this bitty courtyard, an old wooden door sits ajar. Nadia glances over, her eyes going to the weathered sign with a wishbone on it and the tiny card in the window, hand lettered reading *Caster Paraphernalia Within*. She smiles at the shopkeeper who nods back, the caster witch adjusting her glasses. Elise lowers the parasol, and they head inside the tearoom.

It's a cozy space with only ten tables, the reason they tend to favor this one. At this hour, the shop is populated by only a pair of women in the corner and a gentleman right inside the door whose companion is a book. The eight or so empty tables are still covered with pink tablecloths and set with small plates, cloth napkins, and vases with desert brush blooming in them. Along the back wall, a marble and iron counter with a glass case shows off some of the pastries available.

The tea room's current owner Atley Bishop rounds the counter and shows the pair to their usual window table facing the courtyard and the Wishbone opposite. The middle-aged woman with dark skin and dark hair studies them for a moment and then fetches a tower of treats laden with scones, thickened cream, dishes of the bright prickly pear jam the shop is known for, sandwiches with egg and cheese and fish fillings, some tiny chocolates with pomegranate seeds on top telling them what the filling is. A second trip to the counter produces a tall, chilled pitcher of hibiscus tea with mint leaves mixed in and a pair of goblets to drink it with.

Before Nadia can even ask, Atley says, "I'm doing well, Nadia. How are you today?"

Elise chuckles.

"Tired from our studies."

Atley lowers her voice. "Perhaps I should recommend waiting as the tea crowd thins out and you can relax fully."

Nadia makes full eye-contact with the woman. She recalls briefly the first caster-thing she learned and opens herself up to the witch's mind. *The man is a member of the Church of Humanity. The women are human and harmless, but you must be cautious in your conversation,*" she says in witchspeak.

Quietly, Nadia says, including Elise, "I don't believe we have any more obligations today. We intend to take our time."

Atley nods and returns to the counter.

After a few minutes Elise whispers, "What did I miss?"

All Nadia whispers back is, "C-O-H."

Elise pours the tea for both of them, and they each begin loading their plates with scones and cream and jam to start. The sweet cool jam tastes marvelous in the day's heat. The two sit in companionable silence and work their way through the scones.

As Elise reaches for the tiny sandwiches, the two ladies in the corner get up and prepare to check out. The shop will be closing in about ten minutes. The gentleman by the door stands, leaves a few coins on his table, and tips his hat at Atley. She waves from the counter where she is packing up a box of pastries for the ladies to take with them. Nadia's gaze goes out the window, watching the man leave through the tiny courtyard. She sees him pause and study the Wishbone where the caster witch watches from the window. She blinks and for a fraction of a second, she sees the shop on fire, the whole courtyard burning. The very tearoom she is in, on fire and burning to the ground.

Then it's gone as quickly as it came.

Nadia shivers.

The two ladies head out into the courtyard and down the alleyway, a pink box in tow and a pair of black and white parasols (the current fashion) open to provide shade.

The doors shut, Atley latches them and then joins the girls at the tiny table. Elise hands her a scone while studying Nadia's reactions.

"Did you see it?" Atley asks softly.

"The fire?"

Atley nods.

"What was that? The future?"

Atley lifts a shoulder. "In my experience, desire and intention get tangled sometimes. It felt like just his thoughts and not his future to me," she says. "I hope so anyway."

Nadia nods and they collectively set that aside for the time being. Elise reaches into her reticule and pulls out the letter she was waiting to share with Nadia. The writer is Elise's aunt who works on special projects for several Umbrian universities and the Central Science Entity.

Elise flips through the pages before coming to the third sheaf.

"Ah," she says. "Here. She's describing the project she's working on."

She continues reading:

> *I have high hopes for the winter project this year. We need a few more witches and at least another air elemental, but we finally found our fire elemental and a pair of caster witches strong enough to hold the lines down. We could use a writer witch, but I don't know if we can afford one. They would need to be brought in from Egraria or Matraize maybe.*
>
> *The trouble is the engineering is sound, I don't doubt our scientists' abilities, but we have no way of knowing what will work beyond our atmosphere. The great Halid Koroman did so much to expand our knowledge of space, but since his death two years ago it has been difficult to find someone with the necessary talent to take up his work. The vessel should hold together just fine, but testing it is the tricky part. Halid's idea was to create an artificial vacuum here and test that the vessel could hold the air in. Without the*

writer witch and the extra air elemental, we have no way to create the necessary artificial vacuum.

We need a writer witch to write protocols for such a vacuum and an extra air elemental, so the burden is not placed on the one we have. We don't have a writer in residence at the moment. As you know, writers are scarce in Umbra. If you know of any writers who are looking for low-paying or possibly volunteer work that might change humanity, please send them my way.

Triumphantly, Elise looks up at Nadia and shuffles to the last page. "She included a diagram of what they believe they need." She hands the page to Nadia.

Atley leans over curiously as Nadia studies it. The bulk of the sheet is taken up by a diagram of the vessel they are building. Elise's aunt has written detailed descriptions along the margins of the page. Each joint and edge has specific requirements, and she has taken the time to write them out. Everything from atmosphere and pressure requirements to the integrity of the materials is scribbled in those margins.

Nadia raises her eyebrows at the descriptions and says to Elise, "Too bad you're not a writer. You'd love doing this."

Elise barks a laugh. "I would, there's a lot of math involved," she chuckles.

"It always amuses me that you're called 'writer witches' when it's such a limiting term," Atley says. "Then again it's the same with seers."

Elise shrugs. "Historical traditionalism."

Naida shakes her head. "I need a proper teacher." She says to Elise, "No offense but I can't get proficient on secondhand knowledge."

"That's fair," Elise says.

"Have you spoken to Aagard about this?" Atley says, referring to the new dean of her school. Arnvør Aagard is human, but she has been sympathetic to Nadia's situation. The issue of course is Nadia's family.

Atley reaches over and clasps Nadia's hand. "Ask her. Trust me."

A shiver runs up Nadia's spine, a chill noticeable even in the desert heat. "I'll make an appointment with her this afternoon. We'll see if she can meet with me tomorrow," she says. She raises her eyebrows at Atley. "Any other cryptic messages?"

"Only that you better send a wire message to Mr. Kaye to get him back here," she chuckles.

Elise shakes her head. "I don't know how you do it,

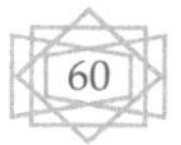

Atley," she says. "There aren't a lot of witches in my family. I wish I understood it better."

Atley smiles. "When I was a child, I had trouble discerning between what I was seeing with my power and what I was seeing in reality. I'm a futurist," she says. "Sometimes seeing the present amidst all the futures is difficult to filter out. But we are taught young that focusing on one moment, one object or image, gives clarity to the whole. Focus on one thing and the rest will sort themselves out."

Nadia studies the spell diagram contemplatively. "Do you mind if I keep this?"

"Not at all," Elise answers. "My aunt would want that."

"We should get back," Nadia says.

Atley rises and begins tidying the table. "I have your usual package ready to go. Plus the extra chocolates you wanted for this weekend."

Elise snorts in a most unladylike manner. "Sorry, I just get so stunned when you do that sometimes."

Nadia shakes her head as Atley hands the package to Elise. They pay Atley for their tea and head out the door. Across the way the proprietor of the Wishbone nods at them as they pass through the courtyard. Elise raises the parasol, and they huddle under it the whole way back up the alley and through town.

The school gate stands open with the gate monitor in the booth to the side. The afternoon has gotten too hot for the monitor to be outside properly watching. The senior merely glances up, waves at Nadia and Elise, and writes their names down in the door log. Nadia and Elise smile and continue through the gate toward their dormitory. The free hour is up, but this late in the afternoon there is no point in going to either study hall or class. The bell signaling the end of formal classes will ring in only half an hour.

Seven

"What do you think about going to Saphlaw with us tomorrow?"

The question falls on deaf ears.

"Aidan," Ethan hisses.

He snaps out of it. "What?"

"Your head's been in orbit since you got here after your meeting with Goliyant," he says. "You haven't heard a word I've said in twenty minutes."

Aidan glances at John, at the three others sitting with them, and back at Ethan. "I'm sorry, you're right, I have no idea what you were saying."

Chloe sitting next to John says, "He was saying that his sister is visiting and we're going to Saphlaw if you want to join."

"Oh," Aidan says, "yeah I'll come with you." And he lapses into silence again.

Five pairs of eyes stare at him in concern. He isn't exactly known for being chatty, but he isn't this silent and deep in thought often either.

"Are you alright?"

He isn't sure who asked, but he looks up to realize he had gone elsewhere again.

"Yeah, just . . . deep in thought I guess."

"Is your writer technique getting any better?" John asks.

The phrase "writer technique" snaps him back to present. John knows Aidan's true calling, but no one else, not even Ethan, knows what he is. He looks around at this small group of concerned friends, all five sets of eyes on him. Chloe and Marnie, sisters with nearly identical hazel eyes, sit with Alex wedged between them and John across from him. Next to him Ethan stirs restlessly, as he often does. He realizes he doesn't have to tell them the exact reason why he's upset, but he can tell them about his struggles with being what he is and they might understand. Chloe, Marnie, and Alex might not be witches, but they understand that enough as anyone their age does.

He sets his fork down and the group takes a cue from him and leans in.

"It's partly my conversation with Goliyant," he says. He pauses to think through the words. "I just don't feel . . . like I'm a good fit?" he says the question in his voice. "For being the kind of witch I am, I mean."

Marnie nods and says, "You mean how you might be gifted that way, but you're not comfortable being that person?"

Aidan nods back at her, "Yeah. Like maybe I'm not supposed to be a . . . uh . . . writer witch or something." He glances at John whose face reveals nothing. "Finding the Spike was good, but I don't know. I just feel kinda . . . stalled."

"We all know what that's like," Alex says empathetically. "Even if it's not because of witch powers."

"What did Goliyant have to say?" Ethan asks in a near-whisper.

The group leans in as Aidan answers, "She told me she had the same struggles I have now," he whispers, not wanting any of the students or teachers in their dining hall to overhear. "I just don't think I'll ever be good at this."

"I think you're being too hard on yourself."

Aidan looks at Ethan. "What do you mean?"

Ethan shrugs, his shoulders loose and pointy since the boy grew suddenly last year. He has the easy posture of someone who doesn't know what to do with themselves and has given up trying. "Well, you know how my mum is always on me to be a doctor," he says. The group nods because not one of them could ever see him being a doctor. "And I used to pressure myself really hard to get good at what I needed to become a doctor. And I'm no good at it."

Aidan works to hide a smile.

"But I'm a witch, and a caster witch at that," he says. "So, I was thinking of specializing in healing, not just for her, but for me too." He leans forward. "I just don't think I'll ever master the science the way I would need to to become a doctor. But I can weave spells well enough to master healing that way."

He wasn't lying and he wasn't boasting. Ethan is the best caster in their class and probably the best student at the school. In every other subject his abilities are almost tragic they're so bad. Everything from physics to athletics to home cooking. He usually can't even get water to boil—without the use of a spell. Which was kind of his point.

"You just gotta work around your shortcomings," he says, shrugging as his cheeks turn bright red at the attention. "Give yourself a break. You'll figure it out."

"He's right," John says from across the table. Aidan meets his trusted partner's gaze. "I'm sure Goliyant told you the same."

Aidan lifts one shoulder in a half shrug. "She said I never have to use it, but should master it," he says. An amused smile creeps across his face as he adds, "She said I could be a caster my whole life if I wanted."

"There's never only one way to do or be anything," Alex says. He is such a soft-spoken person they all hush when he speaks.

Chloe chuckles. "Yeah, it's what we learned in chemistry last week."

"What?"

She looks at him and the blank faces of the others with an expression of utter disdain. "C'mon people, I wasn't the only one in that class."

"Well, I'm not in it yet," Marnie, who is a year behind them, points out.

"True." Chloe explains, "It's what Gallagher said

about path dependence." They might be in the same chemistry class, either for magical or scientific reasons, but none of them pays as much attention as Chloe does. "Thermodynamics, ok? The amount of work done to get from point A to point B depends on the path you take to get there. Change your path and the work changes but the endpoint remains the same."

Blank stares meet her words.

Irritated, Chloe says, "*People*. The way you get there doesn't matter if you still get from A to B."

"Why didn't you just say that?"

Chloe rolls her eyes in typical fashion, her sister shaking her head.

A bell chimes in the distance signally the hour. All of them move quickly to get up from the table, gathering their things as they move along to the next class or study hour or practice time of the day. As Aidan leaves the hall, John draws even with him, silent until they pull away from the crowd and are suddenly alone.

"Do you really just want to be a caster for your whole life?" he asks softly.

Aidan stops and looks around. Both of them have free study periods right now so there is no hurry to be anywhere. The hall is empty, the soft padding of sandals and boots on the stone floor dissipating as the last few students go into classrooms. Most of the rooms have their doors propped open to help with air circulation. The soft droning of teachers begins in the background.

"I don't know," Aidan says. "You know how I feel. I just don't think I *fit* as a writer."

His friend studies him with the gray eyes characteristic of his nomadic people. Aidan stands a few inches taller than John and the height difference always makes him hunch slightly. John wiggles his eyebrows and Aidan glances in both directions. Internally he flexes his power and the Gag woven in the very air around him expands to encompass John. In the center of the spell, it can no longer prevent John from speaking.

"I know you don't feel stable as an anchor," John whispers. The Gag muffles their words so they don't carry down the hall to any unexpected listeners. "If the Spike taught you anything, it's that you can use your anchor abilities, even if you aren't comfortable with them yet."

Aidan shrugs. "It's more of a personality mismatch." His mind goes back to what Ethan said about being a doctor. He thought it would be similar to training to be a doctor and not being comfortable with patients.

"Aidan you're not even fifteen yet," he says. "I know you know yourself better than most people your age. And that in itself is a side effect of being an anchor."

Aidan nods. His partner is right. After all these years, no one knows him as well as John does. There is truth to what he says, same as what Goliyant said.

"What do you feel you are?" John whispers.

He shrugs and says, "The only thing I'm comfortable with is casting." The truth rings in that statement. Pouring power into spells and directing it really was the only thing he felt truly gifted at. This comfort is why Goliyant said he could be a caster witch his whole life if he chose.

John lifted a shoulder. "Then get good at it. Better than Dean Watters. Focus, Aidan. Maybe something will out itself when you're focusing elsewhere."

Doubts fill him about whether he could get to Dean Watters's renown proficiency.

"Don't think about it," John says, predicting what Aidan will say next. "Let's go take a walk and get outside. Yddril will be up."

Outside in the courtyard, the open plateau sky pale with late afternoon light, Aidan shrugs his shoulders and leans back to find the bright point in the sky. There. To the east above the courtyard wall, a bright blue-green point in the shadow of Anax. Their sister planet between them and the sun, a beacon of changing things.

Four hundred years has passed since the dawn of the age of astronomy, when humans learned that planet had as much life as their own. A whole sentient species watching them back waiting on Yddril. Yddril, the name they know only because they communicate with them now. The name of the planet they gave themselves. Before then on Terra that bright spot was known as Turan. But now every human calls it by the name they call themselves.

Maybe he can become a better caster and claim that for himself, Aidan thinks. Maybe John is right and distraction is all there is to it.

John suggests a walk and they head out through the gate together, Aidan's head filled with deep thoughts and new possibilities.

Eight

A knock on the door gets Nadia's attention. She calls for the knocker to come in and looks up to the door of her study to see a young student from the lower boarding school peeking in.

"Hello," she says genially. She doesn't recognize the girl, but she does recognize the job. When she was eleven, she held the same position, acting as a runner for the main school office. The building located to one side of the quad is far enough from the dorms and the faculty offices that a messenger such as this is usually necessary.

"Miss Oswald, you're wanted by Dean Aagard," the girl says.

Nadia closes her pen and sets it in her desk drawer. She closes her books and stacks her homework carefully, putting everything neatly away. Finally, she packs it all up in her shoulderbag and stands. "I'll come with you," she says.

Nadia follows the girl out of the study, locking the door behind her and stowing her keys. Then they walk down the hall and take the back stairs through the side door of the upper school's study hall. Nadia's pokey room is located almost in the rafters of the attic. She doesn't mind it though as the room is really hers.

They step outside and she pulls her veil up over her face to block out the dusty wind. This time of year, the fine grains of sand get into everything and veils are not merely a luxury or a fashion statement. They are a necessity.

Crossing the quad they pass many students, some of Nadia's close acquaintance and others she barely knows the sight of. Elise waves at her but does not stop, heading at breakneck speed for presumably her next class. They would catch up later.

In the vestibule of the main school office building, she slips her veil down and shakes the sand off her shoes. The quad might be paved and there might be some trees and gardens to help break the wind, but the sand still gets everywhere. It's pervasive like that.

The girl leads Nadia into the main foyer and up the

marble steps to the right of the room. The gallery overlooking them boasts portraits of all the headmistresses and some previous notable alumnae. They walk down the second-floor hallway past several administrators' offices to a large office at the end. There the student opens the door to a secretary's office beyond.

"Ah, Miss Wilson," the secretary says. "I see you have Miss Oswald."

"Yes, ma'am," Miss Wilson says. "I'll get back to my studies now." She smiles at Nadia and heads to a small desk in the corner where she sits down and begins working at her books.

"I'll take you in," the secretary says. She leads Nadia to the interior office, opening the door and announcing her.

"Come in, Miss Oswald," Dean Aagard says. She gestures to a chair across her desk and adds, "Please sit down. I'll be with you in just a minute."

Nadia peers around the office, studying her surroundings. The wall behind her is filled with bookshelves crammed with every book she could never imagine. The dean's collection is extensive and extends to the paintings on the walls. She recognizes a Maurice Bishop painting in the corner. It's a small one, but it is impressive nonetheless.

The dean coughs, drawing her attention back. "You like my collection?"

"Yes, very much," she says. "I'd love to know more about it." She continues to peer around and look at the corners for another minute.

"Maybe another time," the dean says. "I'd be happy to walk you through it, if you're really interested."

Looking back at the dean, she smiles and says, "I would like that, thank you."

Dean Aagard smiles kindly at her. She has been sympathetic to her situation though Nadia is not sure why. Aagard comes from a human family and has little to no connection to the world of witches and magic. Still, it is nice to have a sort-of ally in her corner.

"I have taken your request seriously, I want you to know," she says. "And I'm happy to tell you I've gotten you a place in a conference next week. You will need to call your father's man back to accompany you. It's down at Courtthostur Academy."

Surprised, Nadia's eyebrows go up as she asks, "Do you think they'll have a writer witch I can study with?"

"I know they will," she says. "One of the organizers—," she checks her notes, "—a Professor

Goliyant is a writer witch. She's happy to take you under her wing during the week-long conference."

Aagard hands her a piece of paper containing the list of potential participants and seminar topics for the meeting. Nadia reads through it without really taking it in. It starts at the top with some witch topics, like seminars on the Central Dogma of Witchcraft and other less esoteric topics. At the bottom are more practical things like physics and mathematics which are useful to most casters.

Confused, she asks, "But I thought it was against the rules to practice witchcraft here."

The dean of Fernsby School for Girls smiles conspiratorially at her. "But you won't be on school grounds for the conference." Aagard picks up her pen and begins writing a note. "I'll let them know you've accepted and you're coming. Be ready to leave next week."

"Thank you, Dean Aagard," Nadia says.

"Make us proud, Miss Oswald," the dean says. "You're the only student to represent us at this kind of conference. Make sure you represent us well."

Nadia nods and gets up to leave.

"I'll let you know when you can come by and learn

about my collection," Dean Aagard says with a coy smile.

"Of course, Dean," Nadia says.

She takes a last look around the room before leaving. In the vestibule she says farewell to the secretary and waves at Miss Wilson. The girl waves back and turns back to her books. Dean Aagard is a much nicer dean to work for than the old one in Nadia's time.

Instead of heading back to her study, Nadia heads for her dorm. She shares a room with Elise and she's hoping to catch her there when Elise gets out of her next class in about twenty minutes. Their dorm is conveniently next to the building with most of their classes in it. Not all students of Fernsby live on the campus. Some are local to Coreton and live in the town with their families. The upper school makes sure that the students have the conveniences such as a study and a dorm close to classes. The idea is that it makes for fewer distractions. In reality they make their own distractions no matter how convenient things are.

She unlocks the door to their shared space, a room barely wide enough for both single beds and the nightstand between them. Their closets hold most of their clothes but it's tight enough that Elise bought a tiny wardrobe in town last year. She hangs most of her extra winter clothes in there. Being from Umbra, she has a more extensive collection of stylish and functional winter coats than Nadia will ever have.

Nadia drops her bag on the floor and flops down on her bed. Then she sits back up to take off her boots. The quilt on her bed is from her father. She lays back onto the downy cover and stares at the ceiling thinking. The frustration she feels over not having a proper teacher is finally ebbing a bit. She thinks about the strange people she has met over the past year, since she really came to terms with having witchcraft in her. The first couple years she kept denying it to herself. She was forced to suppress that part of herself. It was only Elise who helped her let go of her fears and find a way to practice.

The door opens and in steps Elise, also carrying a bag and looking exhausted. She drops her bag much in the same manner as Nadia did and flops down on her bed as well.

"Long day?"

"Yep. Yours?"

"Yep. I had good news though."

"What kind of good news?" Elise says, sitting up.

Nadia sits up to face her. "Aagard is sending me to a

conference in Courtthostur. One of the witches running it is a writer witch."

"Really?" Elise says in surprise. "That's so great!"

"It's a good thing I sent a wire to Kaye yesterday," Nadia says.

"It's a good thing Atley warned you," Elise says. "How long will you be gone?"

"A week. I was hoping you could come with me."

Elise's eyebrows go up and she leans back. "Is the conference only for witches?"

"I don't know, and I don't really care," Nadia says. "I'm sure there's some diplomatic or governmental reason why a representative of Umbra should be at a conference for witches. Do you want to try?"

Elise laughs in response. "I'm sure there is," she says. "I'll ask Aagard if I can come with you. If I can't go, will you be alright?"

"I'll be fine. I just don't want Kaye to be the only person I know for the whole week."

"Well you'll have the people at the conference."

"Who I won't know yet and will need to conceal my identity from."

A look of understanding comes over Elise's face. "Right because your family won't want you to go," she says. "What did you tell Kaye?"

"The truth, but he won't give me away," Nadia says.

Elise nods. "How can I come to a witch conference?"

"I think everyone comes to these things. Witches, humans, elementals, and even the occasional spirit, though I doubt one this small will see either of those two." Nadia pauses, thinking for a moment. "They have an advanced mathematics seminar that you might be interested in. It's more for casters and writers, but you could get something out of it."

Elise scowls. Her weakness is for advanced mathematics and Nadia knows it. She knows no carrot is bigger than that one.

"Fine, I'll wire my parents and let them know I'm going to be in Courtthostur for a week," she says. "I'll tell them your escort is coming so they don't have to send one. They probably will anyway, knowing them."

Nadia shrugs. "An extra chaperone isn't going to bother anyone except you," she says.

"True," Elise says. "I'll go ask Dean Aagard. When do we leave?"

"Early next week."

Elise nods, grabs her bag, and heads back out the

door.

Nadia watches her friend leave and then gets up to look through her closet. Her to-do list suddenly got very long indeed.

Nine

The day the conference opened Aidan woke up at a normal time for the first time in a long time. With the conference going on and being hosted partially by the school, most classes had been suspended for the week with very rare exceptions. John still needed to attend his binary planets lecture later in the week, but most of the crew's classes were all canceled.

The first event of the conference takes place in the afternoon of the first day. A casual tea allows for attendees to introduce themselves and get acquainted with the schedule and the school grounds. Goliyant was correct in saying that this is one of the smaller conferences. What they lack in size they make up for in diversity. Among the attendees are no less than three writer witches, the anchor witch Goliyant promised, and their surprise guest: a fire elemental. The latter is the person Aidan has the most desire to meet.

"Then go introduce yourself," John whispers. "And stop staring. It's rude."

Aidan takes a sip of tea. He glares surreptitiously at John before setting his cup on its saucer without so much as a clink. They are standing at the side of the reception room, casually watching their colleagues and classmates socializing. Aidan has never been the most comfortable among strangers, mostly because of his status. The idea of meeting strangers is unnerving.

"I'll come with you if you want. Just to get you to stop brooding."

Aidan lets out an exasperated breath. "Fine. Let's go talk to him."

They find a place to set down their teacups on the side table and cross the room cautiously and not at all hurriedly. A few greetings and a couple minutes later, they come up to the fire elemental. Aidan extends a hand and he shakes it.

"I'm Aidan Montgomery. This is my casting partner John Blestone."

John extends his hand and gets a shake from the elemental as well.

"Grappley," the elemental says. "Pleasure."

"I am a caster, but my partner is a writer," John says.

Grappley raises an eyebrow at Aidan. He says softly, "But you aren't really, are you." It was not a question.

Aidan's expression mirrors the elemental. "No, but it's not common knowledge." His eyebrows come down. "How did you know?" he asks softly.

"Elementals feel the differences in witches," he says with a shrug as if he is describing the weather.

"That's so unfair," John grumbles under his breath.

Grappley stairs wide-eyed at John. Then he bursts out laughing. "I've never been envied for that before."

"Really? I thought everyone would want to be a fire elemental."

"Some people do," Grappley concedes. "Some despise us, and some fear us." He shrugs. "People tend to fear what they don't understand."

Aidan's glance circulates the room. No one is paying them any attention. They are being ignored in favor of the social graces. "Are you presenting?" Aidan asks.

Grappley tilts his head to the left in an awkward nod. "Yes, on elemental magic and fire casting," he says. "You might find it interesting if you work as a caster."

"I'm working as a writer," Aidan says softly.

"Though I'm no good at it."

"Then you should come. Both of you."

Aidan exchanges a glance with John who gives him a look that says "it's your call."

"Thank you," Aidan says. "I think we will. Will you be giving us a demonstration of your elemental skills?"

Grappley chuckles. "I will, but it will be at night and in the desert. I don't need to burn down any buildings this week," he says with a glint of mischief in his eye.

He is about to ask what Grappley means when Goliyant approaches them. She nods respectfully to Grappley and says to Aidan, "I see you met our special guest." She shakes Grappley's hand as she says, "It's an honor to have an elemental with us. We'll be the envy of the quarterly meetings."

Grappley's eyebrows go up. "Thank you," he says. "I feel very welcome here."

"If you don't mind me stealing Aidan and John, there is someone I would like them to meet," she says.

Grappley nods differentially to Goliyant. "Nice meeting you. I hope we'll talk again later."

"I hope so too."

Aidan follows Goliyant across the reception room with John close to him. The room is slowly starting to empty with the ending of the tea hour. There are maybe a dozen people left between the local students and the visitors. Some of the visitors and students have left in groups to explore the grounds and the city. He had overheard one group wishing to visit the hot spring farms at the center of town. Courtthostur is not known for much, but it is known for that.

Goliyant leads them up to a tall man with green eyes and dark hair. His skin is pale and betrays his upbringing in one of the northern countries, whether that is Umbra or another country. He sets his teacup back in its saucer and sets the saucer on the table as they approach. A girl with dark hair and vibrant blue eyes stands next to him, her eyes widening when she gets a look at Aidan. She too sets down her teacup as they approach.

The man wears the traditional robes of a scholar over his more modern suit. He extends a hand, the robe's bat sleeve falling back to reveal long fingers. Aidan takes the hand and immediately feels a jolt of recognition he had never felt before.

"Aidan, I would like you to meet High Caster Wilhelm Martinsson. Wil, I would like you to meet Aidan Montgomery." Goliyant does the introductions cordially.

"Miss Oswald, I'm surprised you stayed. I thought

your companion went off with a group of casters."

The girl laughs and says, "Yes, Elise went with a bunch of math witches to discuss some equation or other they were talking about. I like math, but it's over my head I'm afraid."

"Miss Oswald discerned who and what I am, as I suspect she has with Aidan here," Wilhelm Martinsson explains.

A look of pure surprise crosses Effie Goliyant's face. "Miss Oswald, you are full of surprises. I thought you were untrained."

"I am," she says. "But even I can see the massive spell surrounding Aidan," she says with wide eyes. "I'm not a seer, but the density of the spell is a little obvious even to me."

"Well, it's obvious to a writer anyway," Goliyant says. "I can see it as well, but I doubt anyone who is not a practiced writer witch would see it clearly."

"I'm not practiced though," she says.

"No, but we'll figure you out soon I hope," Goliyant answers. "In any case, Miss Oswald, this is Aidan Montgomery and his partner John Blestone. Aidan and John, this is Nadia Oswald. She comes to us from Fernsby for the week."

Aidan and John both shake hands with Nadia and they exchange pleasantries.

"You're a writer witch," Aidan says. It's not a question. As Goliyant said, only a writer witch would see through the spell.

"Yes," Nadia answers. "It's complicated though."

"I know the feeling," he says.

"Miss Oswald, perhaps John can take you on a tour of the grounds. I know Aidan and Wil have much to discuss," Goliyant says.

John smiles at Nadia and says, "Come on. We know when we're not wanted." He offers his arm to Nadia who takes it. Aidan shakes his head watching them leave the room, John already making her laugh again.

"Let's go to the faculty sitting room. We won't be disturbed there at this time of day," Goliyant says.

Surprised but grateful, Aidan follows Goliyant out of the reception room and down the hallway, Wilhelm Martinsson falling into step beside him. He doesn't know what this conversation will bring. He just knows the jangly presence of an anchor walking next to him is enough to give him hope. Hope that he might finally understand who he is supposed to be.

Ten

By the third day of the conference, Nadia had gotten into the routine of the meeting. Almost everyone would show up to the morning main speaker, and indeed the session lead by the fire elemental Grappley was packed that morning, then they would break out into small groups held in classrooms in the upper level of the main school. The first day Nadia was overwhelmed by the sheer amount of sessions available at such a small meeting, but now she planned ahead the evening before to map out how she wanted to spend her day. Which is how she found herself in a late-morning lecture on the Vacancy Principle, a tenet of the Central Dogma of Witchcraft that she embodies.

"As we know the human aspect is shared by all, even distantly by spirits," the speaker droned on. She wished he had a more interesting voice. "And the incursion of magic on a human, given by a witch, will reside for days sometimes. And in the case of the witch's death, a human will pick up the magic of the witch they are in contact with."

Someone raised a hand to ask a question about the validity of a spirit having human aspects. Nadia tuned out the ensuing debate not having a strong opinion one way or the other. Having met two different elementals and observed a few spirits in her time, she knows more than anyone that the classification system anthropomorphizes all beings to a human perspective. Or maybe a witch perspective. Either way, the arbitrariness sometimes bothers her.

"Has anyone here received their witch's gifts from the passing of another witch?"

After one or two others raise their hand, Nadia tentatively raises hers. The other two witches, a girl who comes from the south and a boy who lives and works at the school, glance back at her. The speaker is acquainted with both of them and nods knowingly. To Nadia, he looks intrigued.

"Miss . . . ?"

"Oswald. Nadia Oswald," she says. The boy who

raised his hand looks at her like lightning just struck him. And for a moment she thinks he looks familiar. But then their speaker approaches her, leaving a distance between them to speak.

"Miss Oswald, may we ask how you came about your abilities?"

She sits up in her seat, knowing that the story can upset people. "I was ten years old. I witnessed the death of a witch," she says.

"Can you give us more detail?"

Nadia lets out a tight breath. "He was murdered. Right in the middle of the street of my hometown," she says in a rush. "I held his hand as he died. I didn't want him to be alone and I didn't know what would happen."

Rather than press further, the speaker nods, sympathy on his face, and steps back to the front of the room. The rest of those in attendance, seated in a circle, either glance at her surreptitiously or openly stare. The boy looks at her with a sharp intensity that only makes the recognition more prominent. She can't quite place the face, but he looks so familiar.

The rest of the session drags by with the same droning voice, at first using her experience as an example and then going into other historic cases. Nadia is so deep in thought she almost misses the bell signally the end. At that point the boy approaches her and waits for her to get up. She picks up her bag and stands to face him.

"Are you from Avita Spring?" he asks.

Surprised, she says, "Yes I am."

"Do you recognize me?"

"A bit, but I can't quite place you."

"I'm Ethan Iridasia. We used to play together as children."

The recognition shoots through her like fire. Her long-lost best friend is standing right in front of her and talking to her. She drops her bag back on her chair and throws her arms around him. "Ethan!"

He hugs her back with as much ardor. "I thought you forgot about me!"

"Never. My mom . . ."

"Say no more."

They pull back from the hug and Nadia gathers her bag back up.

"There's a sitting area down the hall. Do you have a few minutes to catch up?" he asks.

"Of course!"

Ethan leads her down the hall to an area that widens off the main corridor. There, a scatter of comfy couches and small side tables pepper the space. A side server table bears fresh tea and some snacks for those who chose to lounge there. Ethan asks if she wants some tea and pours it for her when she says yes. They take seats on adjacent couches and drink and begin to catch up.

"I'm so sorry for never writing," Nadia says. "I never knew where you were."

Ethan nods sympathetically. "I knew how your family was even before I became a witch," he explains. "So I never expected to see you again." He pauses for a moment. "Did you meet Aidan Montgomery?"

"Yes, I did on the first day."

"His uncle was there when you got your power."

The name *Montgomery* flickers through her mind. The name badge the patrol officer wore. "His uncle spoke to me."

"Yes," Ethan said. "That's how I knew you got your power. Your name wasn't in the papers, but Aidan said it was the Oswald girl. I knew it was you."

"No one is supposed to know," she says slowly.

"I'm sure some of the witch community know, but I don't believe it is known among humans," he says reassuringly. "I only know because of Aidan. And he only told us because we are his friends."

Nadia nods. "I have friends like that. Well, one anyway. And she's here with me somewhere."

"She's a witch?"

She shakes her head. "I'm one of only a couple witches at Fernsby. Magic is strictly forbidden there," she explains. "Elise is an open-minded human who has been helping me since I got to the school. Without her I wouldn't know any magic at all."

"A very good friend then."

Nadia nods in agreement. "What about you though? Do you have a casting partner?"

"Not really, I mostly work on my own," he says. "My family moved to Saphlaw so I could study here. None of them have magic of course." Nadia knew that. His sister was a talented musician back when they were children. And his parents ran a successful bakery back in Avita Springs. She wonders if the same things are true now.

"How are they? How is Tanya?"

"She's at the music conservatory in Saphlaw," he says. Nadia's surprise must have shown on her face. "I know, she is as much of an over-achiever as I am."

Nadia chuckles. "I take it you're going to be a doctor?"

Ethan shrugs one of his shoulders. He leans back in his seat, his whole body loose but tense at the same time. "I don't think so," he says. "Turns out I don't have the aptitude for science that I need. I think I'm going to try and be a healer instead."

"Oh wow!"

"Yeah," he says sheepishly. "I'm working on it. It's not easy to learn."

"I imagine not," she says. "But I think you can do it."

Ethan raises his eyebrows. "You think so?"

Nadia shrugs. "Back when we were children, you were always very determined. Look how you got your power in the first place," she points out.

"True." A look comes over his face. "Does your mother know about you?"

A dark look passes over Nadia's face. "I think you know better than anyone what would happen if she found out," she says. "But I think my father might know. His man knows and won't say. But I think he knows and is protecting me."

Ethan nods thoughtfully. "And with your father in politics now, are you the dark family secret?"

"Probably," she says laughing.

"I'm not surprised."

"You wouldn't be."

Nadia looks up to see Elise walking in with a small group of witches. She looks like she is in her element, despite being the only one in the group without witch power. Elise spots Nadia, excuses herself from the group, and heads across the room.

"Hey, how was your day?" Elise says taking a seat next to Nadia.

"Good. I'd like you to meet my childhood friend Ethan Iridasia," Nadia says.

Ethan extends a hand to Elise who looks very surprised. "As in *the* Ethan?"

"Yes."

"Wow. I'm glad you found each other!"

"Me too," Ethan says with a smile at Nadia. "It's been far too long." He suddenly sits up straighter seeing another group come into the room. "Oh there's my friends. I want you to meet them."

Seeing Aidan and John in the group, Nadia raises her eyebrows. So no matter what she would have met them. From the nature of the spell, she can tell the rest of the group probably doesn't know Aidan is an anchor. And from what she garnered in the earlier conversation, he must be known as a writer witch around here.

Ethan makes the introductions, Nadia saying she already met Aidan and John, and a few of them go to get tea before joining them.

"This is wild that you two knew each other back in Avita Spring," a girl named Chloe says. "What are the odds you would both wind up at the same meeting?"

Nadia smiles at Ethan. "I hope we can keep in touch after this week."

"For sure! I didn't know where you were or else, I would have contacted you."

"Same."

"So this means you knew Ethan before he became a caster," Chloe's sister Marnie says.

A coy smile comes over her face. "Yes, I did," she says. "But I don't think he's changed much."

"Elise," Alex says, "you are Umbrian?"

"Yes, I am."

"Did you know an Umbrian professor is here for the meeting? He's giving a talk on their contact with Yddril," he says.

"What?" she says incredulously. "I have to attend this." Elise unceremoniously thwacks Nadia's arm. "You should go too." The look she gives her reminds Nadia of the letter with the diagrams from Elise's aunt.

"I should," she says. "There's a lot of writer work in that field."

In the distance a bell tolls.

"That's break," Chloe says, getting up. She takes her sister's teacup and places both of theirs back on the side table. One by one the rest get up and do the same.

"I have a session on the Conservation Law to go to," Nadia says.

"You keep going to theoretical stuff."

"I need it."

"Alright, well, I'll see you at dinner?"

"I'm with you," Ethan says to Nadia. "I'll accompany you to the session if you don't mind."

With a smile Nadia takes Ethan's offered arm and they walk out of the break room together. The rest of the group goes their separate ways. Somehow, in the company of her oldest friend, Nadia's spirit feels lighter.

Eleven

By the time the meeting started winding down at the end of the week, Aidan had a better grasp of what all went into being an anchor. His time with Wilhelm Martinsson proved to be incredibly fruitful.

There is a lot more theory to being an anchor than Aidan thought. It seems the higher in the witch power hierarchy you go, the less it has to do with practice than it does with simply existing. Seers actively work with their power on a daily basis. Casters lean on spellcraft to enact their abilities whenever they choose. Writers create spells and constructs for others and themselves to use. Anchors seemed to focus on grounding. Their purpose exists beyond the practical arts.

This, of course, is the exact thing Aidan has trouble with. As Wilhelm confirmed, knowing yourself and feeling most like yourself provides the fuel for being an anchor. Anchors help the rest of the world be more like itself. Around an anchor reality is more real.

So Aidan spent the rest of the week outside of his meetings with Wilhelm just sampling some of the breakout talks while his mind wandered. Which is how he ended up in a talk on the varieties of spirits. He didn't have a particular interest in the subject, but Grappley proved to be as interesting of a speaker as he is a person. Grappley apparently had some experience with spirits. Elementals are, by definition, the closest a human can get to being a spirit.

The session wound down and the bell chimed in the distance. Aidan snaps out of his reverie and looks around the room. Across the room, the girl he met looks over at him. Nadia had been listening attentively and asking questions. Even now she heads to the front of the room to speak to Grappley, presumably to ask more questions. Her glance at him tells him he should wait for her, so Aidan stays in his seat. Some five minutes pass before she finishes her conversation with Grappley and heads towards him.

"Hello again," she says.

"Nadia, right?"

"Yes."

"Is there something you need?"

"Yes," she says, hesitating. "Would you have tea with me? I want to ask about your . . ." Her eyes danced around to the spell enveloping Aidan.

Aidan nods in understanding. "There's a tea house just down the road from the gate. We can talk there more freely than here," he says. He gets up and heads to the door, gesturing for Nadia to go through ahead of him. She steps through the door and waits for him in the hallway.

"So you're from Avita Spring," he says, falling into step beside her.

"Yes, my family is still there, but they spend more time in Port Nalrang these days with the campaign."

Aidan pauses. "I take it from our conversations this week your family doesn't know you are a witch." It wasn't a question. She had hinted at it.

"My mother disapproves of witches. I knew Ethan growing up, but I was forbidden from seeing him as soon as he gained his grandmother's magic," she explains.

"That's awful," he says, thinking about how much his friends helped him as he came into his power. He couldn't imagine being forbidden from contacting them.

"She's kinda awful, to be honest," Nadia says with a shake of her head. Aidan studies her with a curious look. She is clearly angry at her mother, but there is a sense of controlled calm around her. It's almost as if she knows better than to lose control over it.

They come to the front door and Aidan guides them out and through the courtyard. They take the turn towards the teashop, and he thinks for a moment. Then he asks, "Why do you have to control yourself so much when I ask about your mother?"

"*Why?*" she asks. Her face turns rueful. "I had a few accidents with my power when I was younger. I didn't know how powerful writer witch words could be. When I first came to Fernsby, I almost set fire to my dorm room." She has a crooked smile as she says, "There's still a burn mark on the wall where the flames were. Elise is the reason I found my control."

"Really?"

"Yeah," she says. There is light in her clear blue eyes as she explains, "Elise taught me meditation techniques to control my anger and my grief. I learned from her."

They come to the tea shop bearing the sign "Cake Break" and Aidan holds the door for her. Nadia steps through followed by Aidan. A few minutes later they are at a table for two waiting on an order of tea and the mini cakes the shop is known for. As they wait Aidan glances around the currently crowded room. They are wedged in a corner which will help their conversation be private. Even so, he will erect a privacy screen with magic that will muddle their words to any casual listener. He just wants the tea to get there first.

A gracious waitress comes by with a pot of tea, cups and saucers, teaspoons, and the rest. She lays them down on the table, setting the teapot on the warmer and lighting the candle below it with a flick of the wrist and a muttered word. Their waitress is a caster witch.

She leaves and comes back with a plate of mini cakes, each with a tiny design to denote the filling within. Nadia looks at them in sheer delight, admiring the intricate detail. Aidan smiles half to himself and half at her. This is part of why he brought her here. He suspected she would enjoy how adorable the pastries were.

Aidan takes on the role of host and pours each of them some tea. He adds the milk and sugar Nadia requests, and gently hands her the teacup. Then he pours his own, adding only sugar and a scant amount of milk, before settling back. He thinks through the privacy screen for a few minutes and then casually casts the spell. Nadia watches in fascination as it takes hold around them.

"I envy that," she says. "I don't have the training to do that."

"You could learn it though," he says kindly. "It won't happen overnight, but you could learn it."

She takes a sip of her tea, seemingly thinking. She sets down the cup without so much as a clink. Then she asks, "Can we talk about your . . . predicament?"

Aidan nods. He calmly stretches the spell away from himself, Nadia's eyes widening as it passes through her and encircles the table completely. "We'll be able to talk in here. We can talk about my anchor witch abilities."

"I'm curious about that, but I'm more interested in the spell at the moment."

"I'm honestly surprised you could see it and the purpose."

"I am too," she says. "I don't always know what my abilities are." She delicately picks up a cake and takes a dainty bite. The motion fascinates Aidan. He eats with girls all the time at lunch, but watching someone from a finishing school and a society background is completely different. Nadia's manners are polished to a level Aidan has never seen.

Nadia looks up. "What is it?"

Aidan shakes his head, blushing. "I just have never eaten with someone as refined as you," he says.

A blush spreads across Nadia's cheeks. "Thank you." The sincerity in her words endears her to Aidan. She adds, "I wish my instructor could hear that." A crooked smile crosses her face.

Aidan laughs, knowing all too well how frustrating it is to not be able to perform for a teacher. "I feel that," he says. "I never do my best in front of my instructors."

Nadia nods sympathetically. She takes a sip of tea and then sets her cup down. "Did Professor Goliyant put the spell around you?" she asks.

"Yes." He notes she said "around" as opposed to "on." "How long have you been practicing seeing spells?"

"Honestly? Yours is the first I've seen," she says. "And more than that, could understand."

Surprised, Aidan sits up straighter and sets his teacup down. "Is that why you wanted to have tea?"

"Partially," she admits. "Also I just wanted to learn more about anchor witches. Until this week I didn't know you existed."

Aidan smiles at her in amusement. He feels so disconnected from his power that sometimes he doesn't believe that anchors exist either. "I understand that. As you probably gathered, the only anchor I've met and know of is Wilhelm. I'm sure there are more, but we don't advertise it."

"How is it kept secret?"

Wilhelm did answer that question. Aidan isn't sure if he should share it with Nadia, but he thinks as a witch she has a right to know. "There is an order of monks and sisters belonging to the witch's church that protects anchors."

Confusion crosses Nadia's face. "You mean the Church of Two Moons?"

A crooked smile fills Aidan's face. "No, I don't mean Two Moons," he says. "There is a church only known to the witch community, a hidden one. A safe space for witches."

Nadia's shoulders slump. She looks like she is sinking deep into thought. Aidan wonders if he made a mistake telling her. But then Nadia's sharp eyes meet his. "How would I find them?"

"Only another witch could get you there," he says. "I don't know any of them in Avita Spring. Or Coreton," he adds, remembering where she goes to school.

"That's too bad."

Several minutes pass in companionable silence as they eat cake and drink their tea. Then Aidan breaks the silence by asking, "So what do you want to know about anchors?"

A smile lights Nadia's face.

"As much as you can tell me."

Aidan sets his cup down and begins to relate everything he knows. They pass the hour this way, talking about their abilities and sipping tea and eating cake. Then the tea hour is up and Aidan lowers the privacy screen. Outside the door Aidan offers Nadia his arm. A jolt goes through him when she accepts.

They head down the block together.

Twelve

When the meeting ended and the campus emptied of extra guests, Aidan caught himself walking through the courtyard feeling somehow deflated. The quad, the fountain, the grove of trees where so many students regularly cluster, all seem oddly empty and quiet. He thought it might have to do with the meeting being over and everyone going home. But the reality is the semester break also began that weekend. It would only be a matter of time before all the lingering students would go home for two weeks and then come back refreshed for the tail end of the school year.

Aidan had made plans to go home to Avita Spring, but his family decided they would take a family trip to Kynis Beach. They had been there several times before, enjoying the coastal region and the vacation atmosphere of the southern end of Egraria.

The great cities of the south dot the coastline of the great Falgar Sea, one of the only bodies of water left in the world. The plateau gradually comes down in elevation until it gets to the cliffs of the southern coast. There the water eroded away the rock until the sea absorbed so much that some parts of the cities became islands. To the east away from the cities, several small hamlets occupy the region where the cliffs finally give way to flatter ground and the sea meets the desert. Kynis Beach is one of those far-flung towns.

Half the plateau makes up Egraria Kingdom, with the northern end kissing the dead zone to the north, the deserts meeting the borders to the east, the Kingdom of Mosnia to the west, and the Falgar's waters bordering the south. Saphlaw and Courtthostur sit in the central part of the plateau. His family would come get him and then head south to the beach. Their journey would take them three days to get down there and three days back. So they would have about eight days to spend in Kynis Beach. Aidan is looking forward to the break.

His family arrived on the first day of the week, just as the mass of students were leaving Courtthostur. His parents, uncle, and cousins all stayed in the town for the night. They would all leave for their journey first thing in the morning. That night Aidan had dinner with the family and followed it with a late-night chat and spending time with John. Their partnership needed tending to. They wouldn't see each other until they both got back to campus.

Over late-night coffee they chatted about the future, both their own and the world's future. The witchwire news contained information about the unrest in the south along the coastline. The anti-witch and the "witch first" movements clashed in the streets of Port Nalrang last month. Aidan's family would be skirting Port Nalrang on the way to Kynis Beach. The metropolis would be out of their way anyway.

"What do you think of the work Umbra is doing?" John has asked over their coffee. Umbra had started working on establishing more regular contact with Yddril.

"I think it would be amazing if they could get it to work," Aidan had said. "I know they're looking for a couple more assets, a couple caster witches and a writer to work with them. And also another elemental or two."

"Maybe we could work with them."

A wry smile had filled Aidan's face. "Maybe," he had conceded.

Aidan is not afraid of cold weather, but moving to Umbra would put him right on the north pole practically. He isn't sure he is ready for that. And now under the light of day two mornings later, he isn't sure he's ready for anything that's coming his way.

He finds himself looking out a carriage window at the expanse of empty desert lands that make up the vast amount of Egraria's plateau. His mother sits next to him and his cousins sit opposite. His father and uncle are riding atop the carriage, dealing with the wind and sun as best they can. Despite the desert around them, the day is quite cold due to the elevation of the plateau. As they get further south and the elevation decreases, the weather will warm somewhat until they get to the temperate regions along the coastline. There the temperatures remain bearable during the day with a slight chill at night. Their planet overall tends to be chilly at night because of the lack of water. Only two seas mark the equator.

The carriage comes to a stop in Skiphagen, a village at the tail end of the central plateau. The family disembarks and makes their way to a local tea house to get some refreshments. After taking a minute to relieve himself and splash some water on his face, Aidan joins his family at the table and sits opposite his cousins and uncle.

"How are your studies progressing?" his uncle asks.

Aidan tilts his head to the left, taking a small bite of a scone before answering. "It's progressing better now," he says. "I finally started working with another specialist." "Specialist" is the family code word for what Aidan can do. Not everyone in the family knows of course, but the people at the table do. And they are aware of the spell around him as well.

"That's good news," his uncle answers. Next to him Aidan's mother and father smile, both of whom know about the anchor witch already.

"Yes," Aidan answers. Then he remembers what he wants to say to his uncle. "Oh I almost forgot. I wanted to tell you I met the Oswald girl."

It takes his uncle a moment to understand what he's talking about. Then a look of realization comes over his face. "Oh! You met her. How is she doing?"

Since the whole thing happened, his uncle had always expressed concern about her wellbeing knowing the kind of mother she had. His uncle always expressed regret at not being able to do anything for her.

"She is at Fernsby," Aidan says. "So she is not learning what she needs. But her dean is sympathetic and sent her to the meeting this past week."

His uncle shakes his head. "I can't believe they sent her to Fernsby. Of all the awful things to do to a writer witch."

"Felix," Aidan's mother says with reproach in her voice. "It's not for us to judge how another family raises their children. As much as we might want to."

Uncle Felix shrugs. He is his mother's younger brother and is the unusual person in the family to have a job in public service. "To each their own," he says. "It is a travesty though."

"I'm not arguing with that," she says.

"It doesn't matter," Aidan says. "She has friends at the school who are helping her. Even if those friends are humans and don't have experience with magic."

"Well that's something," Uncle Felix says. "I suppose it's a bit of a long shot of her going to a proper college with magical training."

"Perhaps," Aidan says. "But you never know how things are going to turn out."

"This is true," his father says darkly.

A silence falls over the table for a moment. Aidan breaks it asking, "What are the developments in the south?" At school he is sometimes out of the loop on what is going on, but even his school and his friends are talking about what is going on. At a place like his school, the idea of humans and witches colliding over prejudices on both sides feels like a faraway problem when he is surrounded by his friends.

"It's getting worse," his father says. "The worst part is not that they are clashing in the streets, but that people who are completely uninvolved are getting caught up as well. Did you hear about the bystander who was killed last week?"

"No, I didn't."

"Well, a young man was killed when a riot started in Port Nalrang. He was just walking home and the crowd got violent." Aidan's father shakes his head. "I'm not sure how bad things are going to get. There is news that the same sort of clashes is happening in the south as well."

"Down in Rebluinia they have been having uprisings in both capital cities," his mother adds. "Pratergarde had a similar riot as in Port Nalrang. I'm not sure how bad things are over in Bellcairn."

The fact that Pratergarde, which sits across Falgar Sea from Port Nalrang, had an uprising as well feels all too coincidental to Aidan. The growing extremist movements are getting footholds in too many places. All around the Falgar Sea the reports are the same.

The family quietly finishes their tea in peace after that, moving along to other less worrisome topics of conversation. Once their tea is done, they gather themselves up and head back to the carriage. When they are all settled in, the carriage begins to move, taking them out of Skiphagen and back into the wild regions between cities.

Thirteen

Several hours go by with Aidan's mother taking a nap to pass some of the time. His cousins do the same, but something about travel has always kept Aidan awake and alert. He will not be able to sleep again until they reach Shepport, the coastal town where they will spend their second night. The following day they would travel through Kurrich and on to Kynis Beach along the coast. Aidan looks forward to the time they will spend there.

When his mother wakes later in the afternoon, almost to evening, she asks him about his schooling some more. His cousins sleep on, so he feels obliged to talk freely.

"Do you know what you want to do when you leave Courtthostur?"

"I'm not sure," Aidan admits openly. "I don't feel

connected to my magic yet. Which isn't helping me figure out which direction I want to go in."

"You're starting to grasp it, I understand," his mother says. She is a human and so is his father. However, his family is supportive of him. Even if the family as a whole lacks the experience of witchcraft.

"A bit," Aidan says. "I was able to use it anyway. It's been a difficult time trying but meeting the other specialist has helped. He gave me some insight into how to self-actualize enough to use it."

She shakes her head. "So strange to think how much witchcraft depends on your view of yourself. I always imagined witchcraft would help you shape yourself."

"That's what I thought," Aidan grumbled. "But apparently that's not how it goes when you are what I am."

"You will figure it out," she says. "But in the meantime, study everything you can to be prepared for what you will be. That is the best you can do right now."

Aidan nods, looking back out the window of the carriage. They are passing within sight of Port Nalrang's skyline in the distance. A hazy line of towers, he can see the lights from here as the evening dims down. Every now and then the sunset light glitters off the towers of

Port Nalrang.

The cities in the south are nothing like those in the central plateau. Everything is modern with steamworks for heating and witchwires available everywhere. Every building has dual power systems, both electricity and witchcraft to power everything. The harmony of seeing the human and witch inventions working together always inspired him. Now that harmony is threatened by the unrest there.

His cousins wake up as they enter the northwestern end of Shepport. The city's gaslights, driven by the springs at the heart of the town, are lit already adding a yellow glow to the buildings on either side. It always reminds him of the brick buildings back in Avita Spring, each building designed in the more traditional way. Every window with shutters on either side and every house with a brick porch.

The carriage makes its way through the streets towards the eastern end of town. They always stay at the Gaslighter Inn on the road leading out of town. That way they can get an early start and make it to Kynis Beach before dark.

As they pass through the center of town, the carriage stops briefly to let a line of protesters go by. As Aidan watches through the windows he sees signs with slogans promoting witch superiority carried by some of them. This protest is likely part of the anti-human movement. His mother squeezes his hands in nervousness. Even their mixed family is seen as inferior to these witches.

The carriage starts moving again and Aidan reflects on how stunning it is to see this movement in Shepport. Though a city, Shepport is small enough not to have large protests on a regular basis. Their presence here only makes the unrest feel like it's creeping closer and closer to home.

The carriage pulls up to the Gaslighter Inn, the signature gas lights flickering in the now true darkness. The gate stands open with a sole footman waiting to open the carriage doors. They are later than they want to be and will likely not get enough sleep tonight. Aidan gets down and helps his mother disembark. As they step through the gate, a loud bang goes off in the distance.

As one the whole family turns to the direction of the sound. A cloud of smoke rises at the far end of town.

"Everyone get inside," Aidan's father says. "Felix, can you get on the witchwire and find out what's going on?"

The group moves towards the inn, his father going

to their driver and instructing him to park the carriage behind the inn as quickly as possible. The man complies and directs the horses around the house down the side drive. Inside the familiar inn, there are several guests gathered at the windows and watching the rising smoke. Passersby on the street rush past heading away from the explosion with renewed purpose. They are too far to hear any screams, but the tension in the air is palpable.

Aidan's father begins ushering the group up the stairs, their room keys in hand. They head up with renewed purpose and leave the other guests to watch the chaos unfolding outside. They make their way up the steps to the third floor and their usual suite of rooms. Aidan would be sharing with his two cousins, not that he would be getting any sleep tonight.

"Do you think it was a protest?" his mother asks his father in a hushed voice.

"No doubt."

Uncle Felix comes into the room just then, his face grim with seriousness. He makes eye contact with Aidan's father and mother and shakes his head in disbelief.

"What is it?"

"They bombed the witch protest."

There was no need to explain who "they" was.

"We should leave before dawn," Uncle Felix adds. "I've asked Morrison to be ready." Their driver would likely not be sleeping much either. But Nikolas Morrison is not their only driver. They always travel with two so they can trade off if necessary. Morrison took them the last way from Skiphagen, but Jack Sheilds drove them to Skiphagen.

"We should get as much rest as we can," his mother says. She eyes Aidan but begins directing his cousins into the adjoining bedroom. She knows Aidan will not be sleeping with all of this. Aidan is the only witch in their party.

"Aidan, you should try to rest," his father says.

"I won't be able to tonight."

His father nods in understanding. "You can sit up out here then," he says, indicating the sitting room.

"I think I will. Let me wash up."

Aidan goes into the adjoining bedroom where his mother is herding the cousins to bed. Kenal is not putting up much of a fight, but Ferdinand is. The younger of the two, Ferdinand keeps demanding to know why Aidan can stay up and he can't. Aidan shakes his head and goes to splash water on his face. The indoor water in this place is fed from hot springs and always smells like sulfur a bit. He takes the opportunity to relieve himself and then heads back to the sitting room. His cousins are no longer protesting going to bed.

In the sitting room Aidan finds his uncle and father in deep conversation. When Aidan walks in, his father looks up and says, "The bombing killed several protestors. I think we're not going to have much of a vacation."

"Should we turn back?" he asks.

His father differs to Uncle Felix. The patrol officer looks thoughtful for a moment. "I would say we should cut the trip short, but we should go back by the West Cliff Road." Despite its name, it is not exactly on the West Cliff of the plateau. It is within ten miles of it and connects to the cliff towns, which is the reason for its name.

"We'll have to go out almost to Kynis Beach to get there. And it will take two days longer."

"I think we should go out to Kynis Beach and take the Western Climb to Squall's End. It will take six days to travel back, but it might be worth it to skirt all the cities completely."

Aidan's father nods. "Good," he says. "I think we'll

rest a few days at Kynis Beach before heading for the Climb."

"What do you think Aidan?"

"I think avoiding the cities is a good idea." After a moment he asks, "Will someone ride with me back to Courtthostur?"

"Yes, I think we'll figure that out later," his father answers.

Then his uncle yawns spectacularly. "I think we should all get some rest. Aidan, try to sleep."

"I'll try."

His mother comes back into the sitting room, closing the bedroom door softly behind her. Then she kisses Aidan on the cheek and wishes him goodnight. The three adults go into the two other bedrooms, their doors shutting behind them.

Aidan goes to the window and looks out, seeing the smoke in the distance and catching an occasional glimpse of someone running past on the street. He sits down in a chair near the window. Unease fills him as he waits for the night to be over.

Fourteen

"You heard about the bombing?" Elise whispers to Nadia. Kaye, sitting next to her, glances around the room. No one has taken note of their conversation.

They are staying at the usual inn in Ulheapsa. Mrs. Keys is buzzing around the room to make sure that everyone has enough lemon cakes for the afternoon tea. They made good time getting to the inn and have time to relax and unwind from the long journey. Elise's family's man is seeing to the horses and their rooms. He would join them shortly. Though Nadia did not know Mr. Hughes well, he had proved helpful during their time in Courtthostur and had been a good companion for Kaye.

The sitting room is unusually packed this afternoon. No less than two dozen patrons sit around the various tables and chairs. Nadia has a feeling that some of these people are coming north from the coastal region to get away from the unrest down there. As such she worries about being overheard and anyone finding out she is a witch. Mrs. Keys gave them a small alcove near the back of the room to give them some semblance of privacy.

Nadia leans back in her seat. Hughes crosses the room and takes his seat with them. Kaye pours him some tea and hands over a scone or two. Silence passes for a few minutes before Nadia answers Elise's question.

"I heard one of the other patrons talking about it earlier," she whispers. "They attacked the witches' protest?"

"Yes," Hughes says. "Someone got into their group and planted a bomb before getting away."

Kaye looks around as Elise says, "I guess we should be careful."

Around the room, the other patrons all seemed to be in quiet conversation as they are. The unrest in the south is weighing on everyone. Even up this far north where they are close to the Waste and the border with Umbra, the rumors are already flying around.

"We should discuss this later," Kaye whispers.

One glance across the room told Nadia the reason for his concern. Three young men wearing patches from the Church of Humanity sit at a table together. They are deep in conversation but keep looking around the room like they are searching for someone.

Mrs. Keys comes over to them. She says, "Is there anything else I can get for you four?"

They tell her they are fine and ready to go up to their suite. She clears the teapot and the remaining cakes from the table. As casually as possible, they make their way through the room and to the stairs. Nadia avoids eye contact with the trio from COH until she steps onto the stairs. Then she looks back over her shoulder to see one of them staring intensely at her. She can't make out if it's because she is an Oswald or because she is a witch. Either prospect frightens her.

Once inside their suite, Nadia relaxes a bit. She exchanges a look with Kaye whose expression tells her he caught the man's look as well. Both grim-faced, they take seats in the tiny sitting area with Elise and Hughes.

"Do you think anyone will be safe if things get worse?"

"Not really," Nadia answers Elise's question. "I think they're escalating."

"You must be careful," Kaye says. "Your father wouldn't like it if you put yourself in danger."

Elise looks thoughtful. "But what if she takes herself out of danger?"

"What do you mean?"

"I mean what if she goes to Umbra for the rest of her schooling?"

"You mean leave Fernsby?" Nadia asks.

"You could live with my family," Elise says. "I don't think they would mind." She looks to Hughes for confirmation.

"I don't think they would mind if you were going to come home as well," he says. "Which I imagine is the idea, isn't it?"

"Yes."

Nadia shakes her head. "I'm not sure my family, either my mother or my father, would acquiesce to the idea."

"Your mother is the obstacle, as you know," Kaye answers.

Nadia tilts her head and looks out the window. The view from their suite looks over the courtyard with its two large lemon trees. The sun is setting though and shadows cast across them, drowning them in twilight. She leans back in her chair and sighs.

"I don't know," Nadia says finally. "It's a big thing

to move to another country as you know." Elise smiles sympathetically. She has been living outside her country since she was seven. She came to Fernsby long before Nadia did.

A loud bang echoes through the building, filtered up through the door. The group exchanges looks. Shouting could be heard from the courtyard below.

"Stay here," Kaye says with a glance at Hughes. "I'll go check."

Tension fills the room as they wait. Elise reaches over and squeezes Nadia's hand as they watch a scuffle in the courtyard below. The shouting grows louder and Hughes suggests they move away from the windows. Nadia gets up to accommodate that when Kaye returns.

"The COH men have started a fight and managed to kill a witch in the process," he says grimly. "The patrol is on its way, but I suggest we leave at the first opportunity."

Hughes takes peeks through the window, Nadia and Elise looking at each other in concern. Then Hughes says, "We may have to wait till dawn. The patrol is here already."

Muffled voices begin filtering up through the stairwell to their door. Kaye pokes his head out in the hallway only to be rebuked by a patrol officer.

"Stay in your rooms please. We will be coming through and asking questions shortly."

Kaye nods at the unseen man and shuts the door. He lights a lamp in the corner and then goes to shut the curtains. The room goes from the dimness of twilight to the golden light of the lamp. Kaye lights a few more so they can see adequately. He does not sit down but does encourage both Nadia and Elise to do so. To Nadia he says, "Be careful what you say to them. Just give them your name and no information on your status."

Nadia's jaw clenches in concern. He means not to tell them she is a writer witch. It would immediately involve them, even if they are not involved in the murder below.

An hour passes before a rap on the door precedes the voice of Mr. Keys. Kaye opens the door to find Mr. Keys and two patrol officers outside. One is a detective by the looks of him.

"May we come in?" he asks.

Kaye moves aside and signals for them to come through. Once inside the room, they shut the door and ask the girls not to get up.

"We only have a few questions," the detective says.

The second officer has a notepad for writing down their answers. "Let's start with your names."

Kaye goes around the room making introductions, explaining their relationships to each other. The detective pauses when he says Nadia, no doubt seeing the resemblance to her father's images that have been plastered all over the southern regions for the upcoming election.

"Where were you all during the attack downstairs?"

"We had come up to our rooms," Kaye says. "The girls are tired from our journey and need rest."

The detective nods at Kaye's response and the officer scrawls down their answers. "And what is the nature of your travel?"

"The girls are returning to their school in Coreton after a short trip to Courtthostur."

"Miss Oswald," he says. "And why were you in Courtthostur?"

Nadia pauses, not sure how honest she should answer. In the end all she says is, "I was sent to an academic conference by our dean. I asked that Elise go with me."

"And Miss Chulyin. What sort of conference was it?" he says, directing his next question at Elise. Her surname is one of the lesser-known family names. Her mother chose it for her so Elise's connection with the royal family would be less obvious.

Elise smiles coyly. "Advanced mathematics for me and philosophy for Nadia," she says. It is the broadest stroke she could paint. Witchcraft falls neatly under the purview of natural philosophy, a fact which Elise exploits.

"I see," he says. "I think we have all we need," he adds to Kaye. "I would advise remaining overnight and leaving first thing."

"That is exactly our plan," Kaye answers.

"Good night," the officers each say.

"Mr. Keys, would you be so kind as to send up some herbal tea for the girls?"

"Of course," Mr. Keys says before leaving.

Relief floods through Nadia. She doubts they could have skirted the truth much longer than they did. And she is grateful to Kaye for thinking of ordering the tea. She could use something calming. The noise from the courtyard has yet to abate.

About a half hour passes before the tea arrives. The four of them sip the tea gratefully, the flavors of mint and chamomile soothing their nerves. Before long the drowsiness begins to kick in.

Kaye and Hughes have agreed that one of them should sleep in the outer sitting room to be safe. The girls will share one of the two bedrooms like they do at school.

Nadia's head hits the pillow, her gaze straight up at the ceiling. The regular cadence of Elise's breathing tells her that her friend has fallen asleep. She can't sleep just yet, with the still constant murmur from below. They will be up in a few hours to leave though. So she must try.

Nadia rolls onto her side, fluffing her pillow in frustration, and continues to stare at the wall. Eventually she closes her eyes, willing herself to sleep.

Fifteen

The weather in Courtthostur does not change much with the seasons, but the seasons change Courtthostur. As the air turns from dry heat to dry cold, the farms at the heart of the city all bring in their final harvests. The farmers close down their fields for the end of the growing season. The markets become gradually emptier, both of people and of produce. The streets become less crowded as well, as people go from the heat of Courtthostur outside to the heat of their homes to combat the chill air. For Aidan the changing seasons usually signals the end of the academic period. His mind has not been on his academics recently though.

The bombing in Shepport was just the start of things. Three more followed in Port Nalrang and Esaton Cove. The witchwire brought news that Rebluinia's capital Pratergarde also had a series of bombings. The presence of so many attacks across two countries suggests a much more coordinated offensive than previously assumed. Who exactly is behind the attacks remains a mystery.

Witchwire news coming in several times a day has become one of the most attended events. The news goes up on the board, translated by the witchwire and posted for all to see. The board, located on the wall of the main hallway, had to be moved to the main sitting room to allow for the crowds gathering. A second screen was installed in the dining room not long after the third attack.

It's in the dining room where Aidan is sitting with friends when the third news posting of the day goes up. At first no one takes notice, then a murmur begins to go through the crowd and people begin getting up to read the wire more closely.

"What is it?" Chloe asks, craning her neck to get a look.

"I'll go check," Ethan says, leaving their table and heading to the wall.

"I hope it's not another attack," Marnie says softly. They all exchange dark looks, John's eyes meeting

Aidan's. They don't need to speak to know they are both worried.

Ethan's face is grim as he comes back to the table and sits down. "It's Rebluinia. They say they know who is behind the attacks," he says. "They say it's Ecrium."

"*What?* Why?"

Ethan shrugs but Alex, who is from the coastal region, says softly, "They've always wanted control of both of the Falgar's coasts. This could be a move to take over."

Dark looks follow his words. "Would they risk a war for that?"

Alex shakes his head saying, "I don't know."

"The wire also says Rebluinia has insisted Ecrium break off their support of the dissidents and denounce the attacks or face consequences."

"What *kind* of consequences?"

"The wire didn't say," Ethan says.

Unease permeates the air. John and Aidan look at each other, knowing the far-reaching consequences of such a global conflict.

"Was there anything about our response?"

"Only that the government of Egraria condemns the attacks and denounces any outside involvement the attackers might have," Ethan says.

"So only Rebluinia says Ecrium is responsible, but we have yet to confirm it."

"I envy Umbra and their shield," Chloe says, referring to the country-wide shield deployed around Umbra at all times. It took considerable approval to cross the shield and enter the country. Aidan always thought all Umbrians are isolationists until he met Elise, Nadia's companion. She proved all his preconceptions wrong.

Marnie shrugs. "They have their own problems; nothing comes without a price."

"Cheerful."

"So what happens next?"

"I don't know but I know I'm going to be up for the early witchwire," Alex says grimly. His family would be the most directly impacted by an impending conflict.

"I'll wake up with you," Aidan says immediately. A few others agree to do the same. No one should have to sit by themselves through the anxiety of wondering if their family is going to be impacted by a war.

They pass the rest of their dinner with little conversation. The tension in the air has gotten the better of all of them. No country had gone to war in four hundred years. Not since the discovery that Yddril has sentient life. Not since humanity realized there are things bigger than themselves. Peace reigns in their world, but that could all change in an instant over these old petty concerns.

After dinner Aidan decides to check the mail. He hasn't seen a letter from his new colleagues in a week or so and wonders about the holdup. The unrest in the south might be delaying the mail. The witchwire is expanding to include personal communication, but it will be years before everyone has the capability to use it. Letters still remain the main mode of long-distance communication, though they no longer move via horseback. All of the postal stations use the Oberon machine to teleport mail across long distances.

Dalim Oberon was a writer witch and engineer who died about fifty years ago. He used both his crafts to develop a method of teleporting objects long distances. Over the years other engineers and a variety of witches improved the design. It was only useful for inanimate objects, but that was enough for the mail system to work more efficiently. Delays would happen when there was a backup of mail needing to be teleported and not enough machines at a location. Avita Spring has a few, but not enough to completely prevent backups.

The mail from Avita Spring is not what draws his attention today. After their conversation and his thoughts on Umbra, he is startled to find a letter from the Central Science Entity there. The letter bears a postmark from a week ago, from maybe three weeks after the meeting. No doubt it took time for it to get past the Umbrian shield and into the Egrarian mail system.

Aidan heads to the main sitting room and opens the letter. He is surprised to find that the letter comes from Elise's aunt, Kensa Chulyin-Siku. She writes that Elise had recommended him and Nadia as writer witches for a project she is working on.

The letter reads:

> *The project is complicated and we were looking for a single writer witch to help out. However, Elise suggested that a pair of novice writers might be better overall than a single expert. She says you both have talent enough but might lack in experience. We are intrigued by the idea and would like to offer you the opportunity to come and work with us.*

She goes on to explain some of the particulars of the project and what they are attempting. He feels it is

ambitious to build a craft that could travel to Yddril, but the idea is so intoxicating he has no doubt he's going to join their efforts. Umbrians are anything but isolationists if they are wanting to travel to another world to meet their Yddril counterparts. And there's nothing that would stop him from helping now.

Included in the letter is a series of diagrams and formulas they are using to create the ship's airtight seal. It's common knowledge their atmosphere only goes out so far and they will need a way to contain the air to breathe. The trouble is they have no idea if witchcraft will work past their planet's sphere of influence. So the plan is to send a small, unmanned craft out past the barrier and into what can only be described as open space. When the craft comes back, the internal atmosphere would either be intact or have dissipated completely.

Aidan's dark mood from just a half hour ago fades away with the prospect of such an exciting project. Realizing he has already made up his mind to take the job, he goes to find John to tell him the news. The smile feels out of place amid the world's dark path, but at least he knows he can still find things to smile about.

Sixteen

The two letters in Nadia's hands say it all. She is facing a dilemma and doesn't know now how to handle it.

The first letter is from her mother. As expected, her mother disapproves of everything. From the idea of interning with the Central Science Entity, to moving up to Umbra and becoming a ward of the Chulyin family, to her finishing her studies at Fernsby early to do it. It didn't matter that Nadia's aptitude had earned her a place, never mind her mother not knowing about her magic. Her mother wouldn't approve of Nadia wanting to eat a piece of toast. She expected nothing less.

The second letter comes from Kensa Chulyin-Siku, Elise's aunt. The invitation to the Central Science Entity is written on the first page. Kensa sent her half a dozen pages detailing the work Nadia would be involved with, an expansion on previous letters. Not only would there be writer witch work, but she could use some of it for mathematics and natural history credits. She could work on her university studies while interning.

The opportunity is enticing. The holdback from her mother is expected. Sitting in her room with both letters in her hands, Nadia doesn't know what to do.

Almost five weeks had passed since the meeting. She and Professor Goliyant were continuing her studies via letter. It could not be as effective as in person, but it was better than nothing. Even Goliyant had suggested moving to Umbra and getting an in-person teacher there.

In the time since the meeting and the bombings, the attacks had gotten worse. Rebluinia made overtures of war only two weeks ago, and diplomacy is prevailing at the moment. She had a sinking feeling diplomacy would fail before long. Fortunately it was only a feeling and not a vision at the moment.

Elise pops into their room just then. She takes one look at Nadia and asks, "What's wrong?"

"Mom said no. Kensa said yes."

Elise drops her bag and sits on her bed opposite Nadia. Their knees almost touch with how small their room is. "May I?" she asks, indicating the letters. Nadia hands them over and waits while her friend reads them.

Elise sighs after reading the letters and says, "Well do you want my advice?"

"Yes. I have no idea what to do here?"

"Write a witchwire to your father. Explain everything except your witchcraft. He might be willing to fight for you."

"What if he doesn't?"

"Then you're back to where you are now."

Nadia tilts her head to the side, contemplating. "Why do you think he'll say yes?"

Elise looks her in the eye. "Because of the brooch." Elise goes to Nadia's dresser and pulls the small jewelry box out from where it had been stored. The box came with Nadia's usual birthday package a few weeks ago. The brooch itself represented a kind of mystery.

Elise hands her the box and Nadia opens it reflexively. The brooch bears a filigree design, an abstraction of Terra and their two moons Anax and Epeths. The motif of the two moons shows up in most witch culture. Nadia couldn't make out if her father was telling her he knows about her magic. She was afraid of reading too deeply into it, but the brooch sits there in her dresser drawer making her wonder anyway.

"He probably knows. He's been sympathetic in the past."

"He never crosses my mother though," Nadia says. "Why would he now?"

"Just try."

Nadia sighs. "Alright. I'll send him a witchwire."

"Good. Should we get some tea?"

"Yes, because that will fix everything," Nadia says sarcastically. It is their usual Sammday afternoon free hour. "Should we visit Atley?"

"Yes, and we should skip lecture this afternoon," Elise says with a twinkle in her eye. "I think you need a break."

"Oh and you need a break too?" she asks with a twinge of mischief in her voice.

"Always."

"Let's go then."

Elise grabs her parasol, and they head out the door. About twenty minutes later they walk down Arrowwood Alley and head into Sheffield's. The place is nearly deserted, the tension in their world keeping people at home. The only person patronizing the tea shop sits by the window, where the COH man was sitting last time, and Atley is wrapping up her tea cakes as they walk in.

Atley finishes wrapping up the tea cakes and the woman leaves the shop. Atley directs them to the table at the back of the shop and closes the doors, flipping the sign over to deter any additional patronage. They would have the place to themselves. Atley's tension permeated and both Nadia and Elise gathered that she must have something private to discuss.

With the table laden with tea and scones, sandwiches and fruit with clotted cream, and finally a series of small sweets, Atley sits down to join them.

"Now, drink deeply and fortify yourself," Atley says, taking a scone and some fruit for herself.

Nadia takes a deep drink of the strong black tea fortified with milk and sugar. She puts barely any sugar in it as it has to travel all the way from the coastal region and can be very expensive. The milk comes from goats kept in farms in Coreton. The tea tastes rich with these additions. There is something familiar and soothing about it, though she hadn't had goat's milk before coming to Fernsby.

"What do you wish to discuss?" Elise asks Atley.

Atley sets down her teacup. "I know you are looking to leave for Umbra," she says.

Unsurprised at the seer's abilities, Nadia only nods.

"The sooner you do the better," she says. "You're fourteen now?"

"Yes," Nadia answers. Her birthday was a few weeks ago. Elise had turned fourteen three months before her.

"By the time you are seventeen things will be very different in this world."

"My mother has denied my request to move to Umbra."

"But your father won't," Atley says. She sighs. "I'm sorry because I know you will be leaving. And I know what is coming, for I have seen glimmers of it."

"Is it going to get as bad as they're saying down south?" Elise asks.

The grim look on Atley's face is enough of an answer, but she voices her concerns anyway. "It's not certain and I am not a seer gifted at seeing politics. I wouldn't run a teashop otherwise if I were," she says with a chuckle. "But when something this big is on the horizon, there are few seers who could avoid seeing it."

"What do you mean?"

"Here is what I think I am seeing," she says. "Rebluinia will be drawn into war with Ecrium. And with them Ostrein. And of course it would only be a matter of time before Egraria joins, if we do not jump in with Rebluinia." Her political assessment is sound and mirrors the analysis of the papers. "However, our smaller neighbors to the east will have trouble keeping out of it. Smaudal and Pepleona, peaceful normally, will go to war."

Nadia lets out a tight breath. The scope of what is coming finally sinks in. Half the planet drawn into conflict with each other, drawing up sides and fighting.

"Will any stand with Ecrium?"

"I don't know for certain, but I believe the countries west and north of Ecrium will back them. They rely on Ecrium for access to the Connector," she says, referring to the waterway between the western Falgar Sea and eastern Nairock Waters. "They won't dare back Rebluinia."

Nadia and Elise exchange glances.

"My family will want me back in Umbra," Elise says. "I will write again to let them know you will be coming once your family approves of it."

"If they want to keep me out of this, they will have to," she says darkly.

Neither Elise nor Atley disagrees. A secret witch in a family of anti-witch activists is bound to become a lightning rod for both sides. Leaving the country and keeping her status largely a secret is her only hope to stay out of the impending turmoil.

Nadia takes another sip of tea. "Do you think war is inevitable at this point?" she asks.

Elise looks at Atley who shrugs a shoulder. "I'm not sure I would say inevitable," she says. "There is certainly time for a diplomatic solution, but the window is closing."

"Do you talk to other seers about this?" Elise asks.

Atley nods, taking a sip of tea. "Yes, but we're in agreement which is both heartening and disheartening."

"How so?"

Atley's smile is wan. "There are plenty of times I wish I were wrong. Like now."

A grim silence greets her words. It never occurred to Nadia that seers see the bad things as well as the good. And it never occurred to her that they might not want to see some of those things come true.

Nadia's eyes go out the window to the shop across the street. She is thinking of her vision of fire and whether she would want that to be real. The answer is undeniably no, she doesn't. She doesn't want to see the Wishbone burn.

"Write your father," Atley says, clasping Nadia's hand. "Write and get out of Egraria before the war breaks out. Go sequester yourself in the north and learn everything you can."

"She's right," Elise says. "We know how bad things are getting and how much you need to leave. We can go as soon as he says yes."

Nadia's eyebrows knit together. "How often do you cross the Waste?" she asks, referring to the desert to the north. "How often do you get home?"

"Not often, as you know," Elise says. "My family usually meets me in Northpass."

The small town of Northpass sits right on the precipice of the plateau to the north, right at the road leading down the slope and through the Waste to Umbra. There another town marks the passthrough of Umbra's great shield, the place where travelers can enter the country. The idea of not being able to go home for long periods is not a new one to Nadia. In fact the friction between her and her mother kept her from ever feeling truly comfortable at home.

"Shall we head back?" Elise asks, breaking Nadia out of her reverie.

Nadia nods and thanks Atley for the tea. They get

up and Atley hands them a small package of cakes to enjoy back in their dorm. They are wrapped in the pretty pink and white patterned cloth used for all the packages out of Sheffield's.

Together they head out of the tea shop and back towards campus. The crackle of change fills the air.

Seventeen

Port Nalrang. The great city on the southern coast, now besieged by bombings and terror attacks almost daily, sits in turmoil as the Ecrium-backed anti-witch groups clash with local advocates. It is the one city Aidan does not want to go to but is the one where he needs to go.

When he returned to Courtthostur, Goliyant had been waiting for him. She had been surprised that he returned so early, but also relieved. She had received news from Wilhelm Martinsson that another anchor of his acquaintance needs assistance. The kind of assistance only another anchor witch can provide. Unsettled at the idea of traveling right to the very place his family had worked to avoid, he hadn't accepted the duty eagerly. Professor Goliyant had made clear he would not be going alone. She would be coming with him.

Their mission to find the anchor witch and help in whatever way they could was of the utmost secrecy. He did not even relay to his family that they were going before they left. The best he could do was let his friends know he would be gone for a while and would return when he was finished with work. To John, he told the truth. He left him a letter using their coded phrases to tell him the work was of the anchor witch kind.

So with no prelude and no fanfare, they left Courtthostur not even a full day after Aidan returned. They spent the next day traveling south and on the morning of the second day took the turn to that great metropolis. This is how Aidan found himself sitting astride a tired horse next to his professor on another tired horse overlooking the glass and metal skyline of the southern city.

"We'll have to use the utmost caution," Professor Goliyant reiterates. She has told him several times. He doesn't mind as it reassures him that they are on the same page about how dangerous this is.

Watching the skyline he sees a sky balloon rise up from one end of the city and head to the east. The balloons are slow and only good for traveling between the great cities of the south. Though some brave daredevils had used them to travel the length of the Egrarian-Mosnian plateau in one shot, those were the exceptions rather than the rule. Rumor had it the Umbrians were working on a better design to make long-distance travel easy and quick.

The balloon moves east. Aidan watches it transfixed for a moment.

A loud bang goes off in the distance.

The sound could only be an explosion. And there, where the balloon took off from only moments early, a plume of smoke and the hint of fire remains. Aidan exchanges a look with Professor Goliyant, the worry mirrored on both their faces.

"We should get going before all chaos breaks out," she says. Their destination is somewhere on the western end of the city. Far enough from the explosion to appease Aidan's nerves for the time being. He admits to himself he is growing nervous.

"We should get to him before dark," Professor Goliyant says. Then she urges her horse forward and Aidan follows.

About an hour later they enter the outskirts of town and make their way through the streets towards their destination. There are few people on the streets and what few are do not linger. They hurry where they are going as quickly as possible, the air of the town filled with anxiousness. At one point they pass through Grand Gala Square and the rubble from one of the last bombings litters the cobblestone. They do not hesitate and move as hastily as those around them.

From Grand Gala they turn down a pokey side street and pass one of those steam-driven carriages, a sight Aidan had only seen a few times before. He looks on in fascination but doesn't let it delay them. They pass it and head down the side street to a district that is poorer and dirtier. Papers proclaiming the sanctity of the anti-witch cause plaster most of the walls and gas lamps. Layered over and around them are more papers that proclaim the opposite. Every corner they turned on the battle waged, if not with bombs then with paper.

They turn down another side street, this one quiet without a single soul on it. The buildings lining the side are not made of metal and glass like so many of the ones they passed on their way to Grand Gala. These buildings are older and constructed of adobe bricks and stone like those in Courtthoster. A few blocks later they come to a series of tenant buildings and Goliyant leads them to one with a falling down black door.

Goliyant dismounts and Aidan follows suit. They tie up their horses along the side of the road, Goliyant putting an anti-thieving charm on the harnesses. Without hesitation Goliyant heads inside the building, carefully putting the falling down door in something resembling closed behind them. Inside she reads the register, finds the room they are seeking, and leads Aidan up a series of rickety stairs.

By the third landing Aidan is seriously worried for his safety on the stairs, but they keep going to the fourth floor. There, several lofts take up the attics of the building. The fourth door down, the last one in the hall, bears no name but a single letter H. Goliyant knocks on the door softly, not wanting to draw attention from the neighbors.

The door opens a crack revealing a wild looking man with dark brown eyes and graying hair. He is easily in his sixties and shows all the signs of someone who fell from prosperity to poverty. His clothes sit disheveled on his body, consisting of out-of-fashion trousers, shirt, and waistcoat, all in poor condition.

"We were sent by Wilhelm," Goliyant whispers.

The dark eyes study Goliyant for a moment. He croaks out, "Not you, him," indicating Aidan. He opens the door the rest of the way and says, "Get inside, quick."

The door shuts behind them and he turns no less than six locks to seal them in. The room is in a state of chaos that makes Aidan's room look tidy by comparison. There are books and papers on shelves and tables and chairs and even on the floor. Several candles stand at the ready because the building does not appear to have gas lighting, much less the new electricity seen in the downtown regions of Port Nalrang. A chalkboard lines one side of the room half filled with scrawls resembling spell patterns. In one corner a cot covered with a thick blanket and a pathetically thin pillow prove he lives in this dank room.

"My neighbors can't be trusted," the man says in hushed tones. "Let's have a look at you," he says to Aidan.

The man immediately gets in Aidan's personal space, inspecting him in a most intrusive way. Aidan is immediately uncomfortable but is trying not to be rude to this obviously not-ok person. And he was definitely the witch they were looking for. The same sense of recognition he experienced with Wilhelm, Aidan felt with this witch.

"What is your name?" Aidan asks suddenly.

"Huh?" the witch says. "Oh, Howells." First name or last name, Aidan didn't ask. This person didn't seem like the sharing type.

"Aidan."

"Right, sure." After a pause, Howells gets out of his personal space and stands back saying, "Well, Wilhelm sent the right person, even if you aren't a true anchor."

The proclamation comes as a shock to Aidan. "What does that mean?"

"You must feel it. You must feel that you haven't centered yourself yet," he says.

Aidan exchanges a look with Goliyant who just shrugs. "No, you're right. I don't feel like an anchor," he says.

Howells lets out a breath. "I know Wilhelm meant well, but I'm not sure how useful you're going to be." He shakes his head. "I guess we'll make do." He gestures to the space around Aidan. "You need to lift the spell around you for this to work."

"Oh."

Aidan concentrates. He hasn't had to completely dismantle the spell in quite a while. Goliyant steps forward and reaches out a hand to extend her power. With Goliyant's help, the spell crumbles easily around him. He feels like an anvil has been lifted from his chest.

"What am I here for?"

Howells rubs his chin, studying Aidan. "Where to begin," he murmurs. "You don't know much about your power, I take it."

Aidan shakes his head.

"Fine, then I'll keep this simple." He goes to the chalkboard. Howells begins by drawing a circle. "Our planet." Aidan nods. "There are at least six of us that I've found," he says, drawing six Xs at points around the circle. "We all serve to shore up the part of the world we live in. Anchors are called anchors because we hold things in place. We make reality a little more real."

Aidan knew that but not much else. He feels incredibly ignorant and out of his depth.

"Take one of us away and we destabilize the planet just a little bit." He pauses and says, "From what I understand there are anchors on Yddril too. This is almost certainly a universal truth that there are those who hold a planet steady." He puts the chalk down steps back in the center of the cluttered and dusty room. "The thing most people, even those who know about anchors, don't know is that we can anchor *populations* as well."

For a moment none of them says anything. They

just stare at each other while Goliyant and Aidan let that sink in. He turns to his professor who has a look of dawning coming on her face.

"Are you suggesting you can anchor the population of Port Nalrang?"

"Not alone."

"That's why you needed another anchor." Goliyant's eyebrows knit together. "Why not go to another anchor you know has practiced?"

"We're getting old," he says. "All of us are. This generation is getting ready to make way for the next." He gestures at Aidan. "There's only ever so many of us at a time." He shrugs as if he didn't just say he would die soon. "The number doesn't matter. Sometimes it's six; sometimes it's two dozen. But there is never more than a few dozen, the most we had during the last war. And there are never more than that." He adds, "Well not that we know of."

"How many of us are there again?"

"Including you, seven. But we never really know how many because we all hide."

A silence passes as Aidan considers what he is saying. He is suggesting using his power to anchor the population of Port Nalrang. To do what?

"What are you suggesting exactly?"

Howells hesitates, studying Aidan again in a way that makes him uncomfortable. Then he says, "We anchor Port Nalrang to help reduce the violence in the city."

Aidan looks at Goliyant who shrugs and says, "I'm out of my depth here. This is up to you."

Howells looks at Aidan with a crazed passion that says he really wants Aidan to say yes. Indecision plagues Aidan, especially now that he knows he is right that he isn't a true anchor yet. Then a distant explosion breaks through his thoughts. And Aidan makes up his mind.

"I'll help you."

Eighteen

In her dorm Nadia packs her bags. Everything she owns that is fancy or presentable in a society setting is going into her bags. She checks under her bed for her shoes and pulls those out as well, storing them in another bag. She has three total at this point and it is the most packing she has done since she came to Fernsby.

Across the room Elise packs as well. They will be traveling together to satisfy her father's only requirement for attending school in Umbra. Nadia will make an appearance with the family on the campaign trail. Her father is running for national office and her mother demanded that she be on the trail with them. They also demanded that Elise come and meet the family. Elise's family sent Hughes last week and he will be accompanying them. Kaye will meet them in Avita

Spring, rather than make the full journey to Coreton. The rest of the family are in Port Nalrang, waiting for the election and continuing the campaign.

The journey will take them more than two weeks to make. It will be the usual two days to Avita Spring and then another two days to Port Nalrang. They will be there for over a week. Nadia needs to plan for wearing multiple levels of society clothing, everything from a day suit to a full formal gown. Hence all the packing. Elise is preparing similarly though she has fewer obligations to appear on the campaign trail than Nadia.

"All done?"

Nadia shuts her last case and locks it. "Just finished." Four bags total. Two trunks and two soft cases to carry her clothes and other personal items.

"We should go down and have dinner with Hughes. We'll need to talk through the trip."

"I can't believe my mother sent the carriage to take us to Port Nalrang," Nadia says, shaking her head.

"It's a good thing she did," Elise says with a pointed look at both their luggage piles.

"It just means more people to chaperone us on the way."

A rap on the door precedes one of those chaperones.

In addition to Hughes coming to act as Elise's chaperone, Nadia's mother sent a driver and two guards to travel with them. The guards would ride on the back of the carriage and watch over them. Hughes would be riding his horse as is his preferred method of travel. The girls would have the carriage to themselves. The same carriage Nadia climbed into after she first got her witchcraft.

"We're here to take your bags down," the man says. His name is Fain and his companion coming in behind him is Heart. Both Fain and Heart have been with the Oswalds for years, their trustworthiness proven by their alignment with her mother's beliefs. Kaye is always the one on her side, though he is loath to show it in front of her mother. It's her father who keeps his beliefs close to his vest.

Nadia gestures and notices their driver Powell hovering in the hallway.

"We'll need you," Fain says to Powell and the driver comes in. The three of them manage to gather up all seven of their bags and head down the hall with much awkward carrying and a few muffled grunts or swears. Nadia and Elise exchange a look.

"Let's go see Hughes."

Together they walk down the hall and down the

dorm stairs to the side building entrance. From there they take the path through the quad where all the plants are native to Coreton and thus accustomed to the region's weather. A singular arrowwood tree stands tall in the center next to the school's fountain. The main building flanks the square opposite the three dorms while the library and two large classroom and study buildings occupy the other sides. Beyond the square are the athletic buildings and field and, in the distance, almost on top of the lip of the plateau, the school's observatory.

One thing Nadia could never fault Fernsby on is the way they taught mathematics and natural history. They even taught extensively on Yddril. Nadia's class had spent a night observing, looking through the telescope at their sister planet and the small artificial satellites orbiting it. The telescope was not powerful enough to make out ground objects, but it certainly showed definitively that they are not alone in the solar system. The teachers might be harsh and some of the students could be prejudiced in ways that surprised Nadia when she first came to Fernsby, but some of the education they do get right.

Elise opens the right door and Nadia steps through. They wind through the main building to the dining hall where they find Hughes waiting for them. He has a partially eaten plate in front of him and the girls go to get their dinner to join him. When sitting down at the table, Nadia glances up and makes brief eye contact with Nessie Lamont. One year ahead of Nadia, Nessie is by far Nadia's least favorite person at Fernsby. Nessie dislikes witches almost as much as Nadia's mother. She threatened to out Nadia on several occasions.

Nadia turns back to her dinner and begins to pick at the pureed root vegetables.

"Have you heard from Kaye?"

"Not yet," Nadia answers Hughes. "I expect he'll leave a message in Ulheapsa. Though I doubt we'll be staying in the same inn after last time."

"Probably not."

"It's too bad really. I like Mrs. Keys."

"Probably for the best though," Elise says. She takes another bite of her casserole and looks thoughtful. She swallows and then says, "Will we stay at your family's home in Avita Spring?"

"Of course," Nadia answers. "I know you want to see it. I doubt we'll be there more than a day though."

"That's enough to see it," Elise answers. "I just want to know where you come from. You're going to get to see my home."

"Hopefully."

Hughes leans back in his chair, his gaze going wide from the table. Nadia knits her eyebrows together and follows where he is looking. The witchwire readout, a simple glass display set into the wall, blinks out a headline that sends a chill up Nadia's spine.

Ecrium declares war on Rebluinia.

She sets down her fork, her appetite having vanished completely.

An uncomfortable silence has taken over the dining hall with all the students and various faculty and guests watching the witchwire with keen interest. Even the kitchen staff have stepped out to watch the report as it comes up. A rare live report follows the initial written story.

Jane Sherhand comes up on the screen. She reports from Port Nalrang along with her human counterpart Winslow Wilson. Winslow appears to be out of the studio for the day.

"Citizens of Egraria," she begins. "I have the solemn duty to report that the growing conflict to our south has hit a breaking point. With the declaration of war on our ally Rebluinia, Egraria has no choice but to stand with them in this conflict. The King will make an address later tonight about the protocols that will be taken in the coming weeks."

There is a pause. The shot cuts away to Winslow who is outside their broadcast headquarters, a crowd behind him looking upset and rowdy.

Winslow reports, "All citizens of majority age should be prepared to be called up should the need arise. Witches and humans alike, and Egraria's elementals, will be on the list of those eligible for conscription."

Nadia turns away from the screen thinking about all the upperclassmen in this room who would be eligible. Not to mention all the faculty and staff who would be as well. It is doubtful any of them would be in Tier One, but not impossible.

"The sooner your family assents to you going to Umbra the better," Hughes says softly. "Your circumstances will not make this easy for you and your specific power will be sought after."

A chill goes up Nadia's spine. She knows Hughes is right. The sooner the better.

"We should leave first thing in the morning," he continues. "Are you all ready to go?"

Both Nadia and Elise confirm they are.

"We will stay in Ulheapsa, at a different inn from last time," he says. Nadia's stomach sinks thinking of last time. Seeing her face, Hughes adds, "We will be close to the Keys' Inn if you want to go visit. I will accompany you."

Nadia nods. Every time something like this happens, she feels the tiny amount of control she has over her life becomes a little more precarious. Even from so far away, her mother can pull her strings. She wonders if it would be the same in Umbra.

"Get some rest, both of you," Hughes says.

"We will," Elise answers. They had both left a simple travel suit ready to be worn the next day.

Finished with dinner, the three remove their plates to the kitchen counter where staff picks them up.

"I will see you at dawn tomorrow," Hughes says. He says goodbye to them and heads down the hall to the stairs that lead to the guest quarters.

Grim-faced, Elise and Nadia head out of the building and back to their dorm. She had the sinking feeling that both were right about her abilities being coveted and needed for a war effort. The look Nessie Lamont gave her only confirms how uncertain her life is. Her mother still does not know about her abilities. She suspects her father knows but has said nothing. Only Kaye explicitly knows. How long would that hold up if she had to pass a conscription test in a couple years? They start testing at the age of majority. She is fourteen. That's only two years away.

Nadia flops onto her bed. Being out of the country would certainly protect her for the time being. Young writer witches had been recruited in the past. If they did not know about her, they would not be able to recruit her.

"Try to sleep," Elise says.

Nadia nods, knowing it would be a struggle, but it would also be necessary. Traveling is always dangerous but even more so when tired.

Despite the early hour, Nadia and Elise both get ready for bed. They sit up for a while chatting about the trip and desperately ignoring the rising signs of danger in their world. When they finally lay down, Nadia lays awake listening to the sounds of Elise breathing. Her friend is asleep but Nadia cannot sleep just yet.

She stares at the walls wondering how long this room would be her home.

Nineteen

Midnight came at last. Aidan had waited with Goliyant and Howells for hours now, Goliyant having left just long enough to secure them rooms in the inn around the corner. Aidan had amused himself by going through some of Howells's books, much to the man's chagrin, and trying to understand the anchor a little better.

The man who started his life influentially, judging from the quantity and quality of the things in the room, had fallen from favor a long time ago. He too had passed himself off as a powerful caster witch to hide his true nature. It had been mildly successful, but as Howells told him he had been outed as a writer witch in his thirties. That lead to his expulsion from the Royal Witch's Academy and he had been out of favor ever since. Thirty years he had lived in increasingly poorer surroundings until he finally came here.

"And I expect to die here," he grumbled, as he concluded his brief and decidedly biased account of his life. "I don't expect anyone to care anymore."

"Wilhelm cares," Goliyant suggested.

"Wilhelm lives in Umbra. The only news he'll get of my death will be when I stop writing."

And they had let the subject drop. The man is the most self-pitying person Aidan had ever met. The distaste he feels for that attitude is only barely allayed by his own pity. He understood that he could turn out this way one day.

So they stand in the middle of his room, with a space cleared and the rest of the books piled up around the perimeter. On the wooden floors, Howells had chalked out his spell diagram, a circular design with some of the universal symbols used in witchcraft. Symbols for man, woman, child, war, peace, balance, justice, and so on. Each symbol he painstakingly etched and refused all help. The diagram is his own design and he covets it.

Finally, the great clock in the center of the neighborhood struck midnight. On the twelfth chime Aidan felt Howells call his power.

Howells had told Aidan to do nothing but stand

opposite the diagram from him and feed power into it. He did not want interference or help. He would cast the spell himself and Aidan would simply assist.

As Howells explained it, his age makes him a weaker anchor. Anchors peak in power when they are most self-actualized in their lives. As they age and creep closer to death, their power wanes as the bodies seek to let go of the world. Aidan is young and is also not a strong anchor yet. He would grow into his power and peak when the time is right. But for now, he can feed raw power into the man's design and help with this most important task.

Howells began to murmur a string of words in witchspeak. He speaks in a mixture of languages so diverse Aidan does not recognize them all. Umbrian ancient dialect no longer spoken in the country, Verhillian's daily tongue, and even Ecrian he recognizes. But for each language he thinks he knows, there are two he has never heard spoken before. With a hundred dialects on the planet and many more ancient tongues long dead, witches always have the choice of what to use. Howells prefers them all it seems.

Aidan glances at Goliyant stationed on the far side of the room, a scant ten feet from him, and all he gets from her is a shake of the head. Goliyant is a skilled writer witch, but even she can make neither head nor tails of the languages Howells speaks. All Aidan can do is raise his hands and release his power into the ring.

The diagram on the ground begins to glow softly from all the power pouring into it.

Then Howells raises his hands back and they form a loose circle with their arms. Standing there, as Howells runs out of breath, he finally speaks in words Aidan understands.

"Conflict. Instability. Diminish."

On the last word, Aidan feels Howells yank on his power. He fights the urge to protest, or worse pull back. It could kill them both if he fought the tug now. Instead he steadies his stance and leans both figuratively and literally into the circle. He pushes more power than he knows what to do with into the circle Howells has set. He can feel it taking every ounce he gives it. He can feel it working through the spell like a sandstorm in the Waste. He blinks as the diagram flashes for a moment then goes dark.

The flow stops.

Howells falls over.

Goliyant gets to him before Aidan does, careful as he is to tiptoe around the edge of the diagram on the floor.

When he gets to him, he sees the man is still alive, just clearly exhausted and unconscious.

"Get him some water," Goliyant says. Aidan complies as she lays the anchor's head down on the floor gently. Then she begins the familiar cadence of the healer's chant. Aidan has heard it directed at him a few times in his life. All witches who could cast know those words.

He returns to Howells's side in time to see the man open his eyes. Alarm sparks the moment he lays his eyes on Aidan. "Did it work?"

"I don't know," Aidan admits. "I think so."

"Make yourself useful and help me up," Howells says to Goliyant. She calmly obliges by offering her arm to support him.

Rather than getting up completely, Howells leans over and reaches out to the diagram on the floor. Tentatively, like he is reaching out to a fire or a hot stove, he taps the diagram a few times.

"Do you feel it?" he asks Aidan.

Aidan shakes his head, not understanding.

"Touch the diagram."

Cautiously, Aidan follows Howells's example and tentatively touches the chalk line nearest to him.

Surprisingly, the chalk line is warm to the touch, so warm in fact that it feels like a sunburn on his fingertips. He inspects his hand to find nothing there, no discoloration and no harm.

"Good." All the praise Howells gives before pulling himself to his feet.

Howells stumbles over to the only armchair in the place and sets himself down. The chair is so tattered and worn out that for a moment Aidan worried it would crumble under the weight of the man. But the chair holds and he lets out a deep sigh.

"I'm getting old," he grumbles.

"I'll make some tea," Goliyant suggests. Without waiting for a response, she finds the kettle and puts on some water to boil, using a charm to achieve it. Aidan had rarely seen her use her power for menial things, preferring the old-fashioned way as she put it. He got the sense that she had been unnerved by the power in the room earlier.

Aidan lets out a sigh as well. He clears a rickety stool of its papers and takes a seat. He feels tired but not so much that he wants to sleep right then. He does not feel the need to sleep. His mind buzzes with the intensity of what they enacted, the strength of his power having surprised him. Internally he wonders if that is the kind of thing in his future. Somehow it unsettles him.

Howells studies him over the cup of tea Goliyant hands him. "Never really used your anchor power before, have you?" he says. It isn't really a question. They both know how out of his depth he is the moment their power contacted each other.

"No."

"You have a lot to learn," Howells grumbles. "I doubt you're going to get proper instructions," he adds, glancing at Goliyant. "None of us do, really."

The weight of his words sinks in. And suddenly he is angry. "Do no anchors help each other? Have none kept records to be passed down?"

The look on Howells's face at Aidan's outburst is a mixture of bemusement and bitterness. "Of course not," he says. "None of us dares to reveal ourselves except in extreme circumstances."

"*Why?!*" Aidan practically shouts.

"Watch your mouth," Howells hisses, glancing at the walls on either side of the room. "Why do you think?" he continues, roughly setting his teacup down on a pile of books. "We can't have contact with each other after this. If you're wise, you won't have contact with Wilhelm either."

Aidan is stunned.

"Why not?" Goliyant says. It had been her idea after all to ask Wilhelm to tutor him.

"Do you have any idea what anyone would do if they found out just how powerful you are?" Howells hisses. "Do you know what they tried to do to *me*?"

Aidan clenches his jaw. He does know. He just doesn't want to admit how stupid they've been thinking anchors can cluster long enough to work together.

"I see by your face that you know exactly what I'm talking about." Howells leans forward, his elbows resting on his knees. "The Rarity Conundrum," he says, naming one of the central principles of witchcraft.

The Rarity Conundrum. The tendency for a rarer form of witchcraft to replace a less rare form. No one understood what made certain forms of witchcraft are so rare. What is it about being an anchor witch that means only a few of them exist? Why are there so few writer witches?

"You mean someone could take my power to replace their own," Aidan says.

"Someone tried to take mine," Howells growls, clearly not over it.

"Someone tried to take mine too."

Goliyant's eyes go wide. It wasn't unheard of for a witch's murder to be traced back to power theft.

"I was attacked as a child," Aidan explains to her. "That's why my parents sent me away. And we weren't even living in Avita Spring at the time. I'm originally from Aynor Spring."

"Yes," Howells says. "And if they had succeeded your power would be in the hands of someone unworthy."

The words catch Aidan's attention.

"The power goes where it must. It goes to the person who is worthy of it," Howells explains. "I have studied this for years. I am probably the only person who knows the names of the most recent anchors. And if you knew what I know, you would understand. We are the peacekeepers, the balance makers. Without us there would have been war many times over."

"The uprising in Mosnia," Goliyant says. "And the annexation of Verhill."

"Both stopped or reversed because of anchors."

"But not even that," Aidan says. "Also the natural threats."

"Yes," he says. "Who do you think stopped the

flooding along the Connector?"

Aidan shakes his head. "But that was done by casters," he says.

"And one of them was an anchor. One of our best."

The weight of his duties, of his mantle, settles down on Aidan's shoulders in a weight heavier than the spell he usually carried. And he knew that spell would go back up and he would have to hide himself once more. Suddenly he felt the loss of being able to talk freely about this power. Of having someone to speak to about it. Of being able to connect with others about his power.

But there *are* others who do know. John for a start. And Nadia who he barely knows but who saw right through the spell. And his family. Howells didn't have anyone.

"So I should keep my distance from the other anchors," he says. "Including Wilhelm."

"Yes," Howells says. "By all means correspond with the man, but do not visit him unless absolutely necessary."

"I'm supposed to go to Umbra to work on a project."

Howells leans back in his chair, seemingly weighing the words he is about to say. "If you cannot cancel without raising suspicions, then don't. But do not seek out Wilhelm unless it is necessary." He pauses. "And you should never see me again either."

Somehow never seeing Howells again doesn't feel like a loss.

"Alright," Aidan says. "We should go to our inn."

The clock on the wall reads just after two in the morning.

Howells stands as both Aidan and Goliyant do. Aidan feels immeasurably tired, his soul weighted with everything they talked of.

"Will you keep records of your work?" Aidan asks Howells.

"I'm not sure yet. I might."

In that instance Aidan decides he must keep a record of his work. He *must* do something so the next anchor has a guide. They cannot go on like this forever. Too much is at stake.

"We'll leave you then."

Aidan shakes the man's elderly hand, the strength and power in the grip still surprising. "It was good to meet you, even if we will never meet again."

"Let's hope we have no cause to meet," Howells says.

"Let's go," Goliyant says. "Farewell Mr. Howells. It was an education."

They make their way out the door. Howells shuts it behind them.

Aidan feels like the door shut on a part of his life he would never get back again. He mourned the loss. He could never feel carefree about his power ever again.

They leave the falling down tenant building and head for the inn.

Twenty

"There have been no incidents in almost a week," Nadia's mother says. "Those horrid people have gotten the message. They cannot associate with decent humans."

Nadia clenches her jaw, sitting stiffly in the parlor of their Port Nalrang apartment. The huge abode takes up a section of the glass and steel building constructed, in part, by witchcraft. The witchwire on the wall uses witchcraft to work properly. The steam carriage they use to get around the city is partially possible because of witchcraft. And yet, despite being surrounded by the fruits of witches' labors, her mother rails against them at every opportunity.

She shifts in her seat, careful not to be obvious about the motion. Her left leg is itchy but she knows better than to try to scratch it. Elise is out at the moment visiting the Umbrian consulate across town with Hughes. Her cousin has sent a witchwire to her to pick up a packet to be brought back to Umbra with Hughes. She declined to say what was in the packet. With Elise out of the house, her mother had taken to her usual tactics of criticizing everything Nadia does. She holds back somewhat while Elise is in the room, but Elise could see the way her mother's abusive streak sits right below the surface.

At first Nadia was embarrassed. But Elise assured her she had nothing to be embarrassed by. It is Nadia's mother who should be embarrassed. Elise's kindness only endeared her to Nadia more. She couldn't have found a better friend.

"Nadia, pay attention," her mother hisses.

Nadia immediately sits up straighter and draws her gaze back from the wall of windows. She is careful not to clench her jaw. At least their apartment gives her joy. They are on the sixteenth floor of the building, about two-thirds up and their floor to ceiling windows afford a view of the cliff edge and the Falgar Sea below. She never sees this much water anywhere else. And something about it calms her.

The city below has the opposite effect though. The

tension had abated somewhat the past week or so, but it doesn't change the fact that the two sides are still at odds. The Church of Humanity had publicly come out in support of the anti-witch activists. Both the Fellowship of Allkind and the Church of Two Moons had condemned the violence. The choosing of sides only made things worse. And the Church of Humanity refused to engage when asked why they were supporting a group backed by Ecrium. Sitting at the precipice of war, the sight of the city below gave Nadia knots in her stomach.

She sets those thoughts aside to focus again on the room.

One of her parents' servants hands her a cup of tea. She uses every ounce of her deportment training to keep from clinking her spoon. Not that her mother would notice the care. Her mother only notices the lack of care.

"I simply do not understand why we must tolerate these creatures in our government," her mother says. "Is it not enough that we are surrounded by reminders of their power?"

"Heather, I can hardly alienate half the populous."

"They do not make up half the populous," her mother rebukes her father. "They are less than half."

Not by much, Nadia thinks to herself. She would never dare say it out loud, but humans barely outnumber witches. Witches might be in the minority, but their proven usefulness over the years had made them valuable members of society. But more than that, witches are people. And all people are worthy of the space they occupy. She knows her mother doesn't view them as people though.

"I will not have this argument again," her father says. "I have done what I needed to do to win the election. I showed my acceptance of witches despite your beliefs."

"*Our* beliefs, Edgar," her mother hisses. "I don't care what you say in public. We do not accept witches in this household."

Her father checks his pocket watch, his exasperation showing for once. He would never show it in public, but Nadia had gotten used to her parents' disharmony over the years. She knows her father doesn't disagree with her mother, but he isn't as vitriolic about his beliefs. Sometimes she hopes that he would one day be able to accept her. Deep inside she fears it would never happen.

The uncomfortable silence that follows is only broken by the clink of her father's teacup on his saucer. Nadia goes back to staring out the window at the shimmering sea. She thinks about Rebluinia and Ostrein and all the lands beyond the waters. She may never get the chance to see them, but she can dream. In this moment, even being on the water itself, feels like a delightful escape. A place that would calm her and help her feel safe.

"Nadia, what did I tell you about paying attention."

"Sorry, mother," she mumbles, pulling her gaze back in.

"Don't apologize. Simply do not do things that need apologies," she reprimands Nadia.

"Heather, that is unfair," her father says sharply. Both mother and daughter stare at him in disbelief. Nadia can count on one hand the number of times her father defended her.

"Edgar," her mother says warningly.

"Don't take that tone with me," he says. "You know perfectly well you were being unreasonable. Nadia has had excellent deportment since attending Fernsby. You made the right decision to send her there." The flattery seems to soothe her mother's nerves. "The teachers are doing everything right. Your daughter just needs the space to show us she knows how to behave."

Her mother nods, looking over at Nadia appraisingly.

It takes every ounce of her training to keep from shrinking under that gaze. "I suppose we are in private."

"Precisely," her father says. "If she is not given leeway in private, she will need it in public."

"Hmm," her mother responds. "I suppose your posture and carriage have dramatically improved since you first went to Fernsby."

"Thank you, mother," Nadia says. "I'm glad you are pleased."

Nadia's mother nods in agreement with herself, saying, "It was the right decision to send you there. If only to get you away from the witches' influence."

Distantly they all hear the front door open. She can make out the murmur of Elise and Hughes talking as they come in. Before long Elise rounds the corner into the room unaccompanied.

"Ah, Miss Chulyin," her father greets her best friend. "How did you make out?"

"Quite well," Elise answers. "The consulate was an education. I had not thought of a career in diplomacy before now."

"Have we piqued your interest enough to want to relocate here?" her mother asks.

"Indeed yes," Elise answers, taking a teacup from the

servant and sitting next to Nadia. "But I already knew I enjoyed Egraria from my time spent in Nadia's company."

"Quite the life partners you two would make," her mother observes, her eyes going back and forth between the two. Nadia's eyebrows go up. The statement is not exactly polite.

Nadia and Elise exchange a look. "I wouldn't know about that," Elise says. "But we are definitely best friends."

Behind her mother her father lets out a tight breath. The look in his eyes says it all. His wife is a burden and he is unable to do anything about it. Sometimes Nadia pities her father. But in the end he doesn't protect her from her mother's vitriol, so she shouldn't feel sorry for him.

They lapse into silence after the awkward exchange, each of them sipping tea or eating a scone. Nadia looks out the window again at that glimmering sea. She is jogged out of her thoughts by Elise's next question.

"Have you decided on whether Nadia can come to school with me in Umbra?"

A jolt of adrenaline goes through her body at the question. She nearly chokes on her tea but manages to compose herself. Her eyes go to her parents who are exchanging a loaded look.

"We have," her father says. "And we have decided that she should go on the condition that Kaye remain in Umbra with her."

Nadia feels her jaw drop and does nothing to correct the unladylike expression.

"Pull yourself together, Nadia," her mother criticizes her. "You will go to get away from all this conflict between Egraria and Ecrium and all those horrid pro-witch people. I don't want you anywhere near any of them."

Elise glances at Nadia and nods. "She will be safe with my family."

"So Mr. Hughes has assured me," she says. "He brought a letter from your family. They better keep their promises," she adds warningly.

"Chulyins keep their promises."

"As I thought."

Nadia's heart hasn't stopped racing. Could she really be getting what she wanted? Could she finally get the training she so desperately needs?

"I have one condition."

Naturally.

Her mother eyes her with a sternness that would kill most people. "You will return in six months for your father's congressional election. He will win this primary next week and I want you here for the campaign."

Nadia swallows, her mouth feeling very dry all of a sudden. "I will be here."

"Good."

Nadia and Elise exchange another loaded look, barely able to contain their joy. "If you'll excuse us, I think we want to freshen up," Nadia says, referring to both her and Elise.

Her mother doesn't question it and simply waves them off like she suddenly doesn't care what her daughter is doing. Both of them gently set down their teacups and leave the room in as unhurried a manner as possible. Then they make it around the corner and down the hall to Nadia's room they are sharing. Immediately they hug like their lives depend on it.

"I can't believe it," Elise whispers.

"I have no explanation. Something went right for once."

They sit down on the bed and continue to chat and softly laugh about the conversation as a whole. Elated, Nadia finally feels like she is going to get somewhere.

She would finally figure out who she is and what she can do. She might finally find her place in this world.

Twenty-One

The first battle between Ecrium and Rebluinia took place about three weeks after the declaration of war. An Ecrian attack vessel sank a Rebluinian cruiser along the Pratergarde coastline. The act was denounced by Egraria and many other nations. Once again Aidan wondered how long before Egraria would send support to the south.

He didn't have time to think about the conflict though. The school year wound down and he turned his focus from his studies to the coming time in Umbra, far from the conflicts of his homeland. After his time working with Howells, he devoted himself to learning the writer witch work Goliyant set for him. His letters from Wilhelm confirmed what Howells stated, about keeping distance from each other. Wilhelm conceded that they could get away with meeting while Aidan was in Umbra. For the time being, the best he could do is use the correspondence to the best of his ability. The process is, to say the least, slow.

When time came for him to leave for Umbra, Aidan felt relief at being able to go. His family supported his decision and encouraged him to get away to work and study his craft for the summer. They did not fully understand his abilities, but they did know he struggled to find teachers. And they understood that he was constantly in danger. So they let him go and gave him everything he needed. He would be accompanied on his journey by one of his father's men who would be staying with him in Umbra. While he would only be there a few months, the time felt like a boon in the midst of all his uncertainty.

Despite the bizarrely cold temperatures for summer, he looked forward to visiting the northernmost country. Aidan had travelled to Reskal along the coast and had been to Mosnia to the east as well, but he had never been north. He packed everything warm he could find and prepared for the long trip ahead.

The journey north took them from Courtthoster through Avita Spring and several smaller villages until they came to Northpass. The northernmost city in Egraria acts as a gateway of sorts between Umbra in the north, Mosnia in the East, and Egraria to the south. It stands on the precipice of the Egrarian-Mosnian plateau right at the beginning of the Wastewalk, the long hairpin-turning road that scales the plateau. Aidan does not look forward to the Wastewalk, but he does look forward to seeing the Waste itself and the great Umbrian shield beyond.

The Waste cuts a wide swathe along the northwest corner of the plateau, from past the Dent all the way along the southern border of Umbra. The desert region is home to mostly spirits and some elementals who have forsworn contact with the rest of humanity. It's mostly earth and wind elementals and spirits, some sand and fire spirits, that live out there. But the mere chance of glimpsing them poses a huge enticement for the journey. Aidan had not travelled through wild areas enough to have glimpsed a spirit before.

So the day they set foot on the head of the Wastewalk, his mind was not so much on the nerve-wracking drop-off next to him as it was on the spirits that dwell in the lands below. It would take them a whole day to get down the Wastewalk, the slow pace being set by fear. Sam Porter, his father's man, set the slow pace as they rode sure-footed mules down the side of the great cliff. Neither of them felt riding horses would be wise, unless of course the beasts had been down this path many times before.

The evening of that first day they stayed at the Inn Below, an aptly named establishment at the base of the Wastewalk. A certain kind of uneasiness had settled into Aidan, making him unsettled and eager to move on. The journey across the Waste would be two days at least, likely three days, and they would be camping the whole way. The incongruity of staying in a boring, ordinary inn along such a wild place felt disingenuous somehow. Almost like he belonged out in the Waste and the walls of the inn felt confining.

The feeling did not last long. The following day they mounted their rides, freshly laden with extra provisions both for themselves and for the mules and headed down the trodden down stone path into the desert. Aidan felt at last that their long journey was getting underway.

On the second night in the Waste, they sat around a small campfire and ate the simple stew Porter prepared for them. Above them the dazzling sky shown with more stars than Aidan knew existed in the night. He had seen dark nights, but here in the Waste the night was unobstructed by building, by light, and by land. The galaxy cut across in a river of reds and blues and yellows. The bright light of Yddril shown more prominently than he had ever seen. Somehow, staring at its bluish point of light, he felt it could be no surprise that the neighboring planet is populated. For the first time since he was a child, he felt the wonder at knowing there was a whole civilization living just one planet over.

"It's incredible, isn't it?" Porter says softly. Neither of them felt it would be right to raise their voices out here.

"Yes," Aidan answers. "I've never seen so many stars."

"You won't again until we cross the Waste in a few months."

Aidan nods and lays back next to the fire. He simply marvels at the sky and the feeling of the fire next to him. For the first time in a long time, he feels at peace with his surroundings.

The third day crossing the Waste, they knew they would make it to Umbra. Just on the other side of the Umbrian shield, a town called Jarren's Outpost housed the shield guards and travelers making the crossing. They had passed a few travelers coming from Umbra, mostly merchants or officials on business. They hadn't seen anyone catching up to them from Egraria, a sign no one with urgent business was coming through the Waste.

Mid-afternoon Porter comes to a complete halt in front of Aidan. Surprised, Aidan pulls his mule to a stop and is about to ask Porter what is going on when the man signals for Aidan to be silent. Aidan follows Porter's gaze and sees what made the man stop so suddenly. There on a ridge within a quarter mile of them a sole spirit hovers over the desert sand.

Aidan's breath catches in his throat. The spirit's form is humanlike but that is where the similarities end. Clearly a fire spirit, the being's long "hair" flows out in a controlled flame. The body is translucent orange and yellow, the glow coming from it casting light away down the ridge. The being turns, spots the two of them, and begins to approach.

"Stay calm," Porter advises.

Aidan's heart thumps in his chest. The chance to meet a spirit suddenly in front of him, he is more nervous than he's ever been.

The figure stops some twenty feet from them, floating gracefully over the sand like there is no effort to it.

Porter nods respectfully to the spirit and greets it.

The voice the spirit answers with echoes inside Aidan's head. The cadence of the voice reminds him of witchspeak, but the worlds don't sound the same. The words, if they are words, don't sound like the common tongue, but Aidan understands their meaning nonetheless.

"*I sensed one with power,*" they say.

Aidan smiles and says, "I have power."

"*I saw one would come this way,*" they continue. The way they said it, the implication is that of foresight or foreknowledge. The statement requires no response. "*May we meet you properly?*"

Confused, Aidan looks at Porter.

"They mean physical contact," Porter explains. "They want to shake your hand."

Understanding dawning on him, Aidan nods and slips off his mule. Porter takes the mule's reins and nods at the wisdom of leaving the animal behind. Animals are notoriously unsettled by the close presence of a spirit.

Aidan crosses the distance between him and the spirit, feeling the heat from the spirit's being long before he got close to it. Once within distance, he offers his hand to the fire spirit, bracing himself for the burning sensation to come. As the spirit reaches out, he is surprised to find the contact is gentle. It is warm, but not burning as if the spirit is controlling its level of heat.

The voice this time is entirely telepathic in nature. *You are not on your path just yet*, they say.

I don't know my path, Aidan answers.

You will, they answer. *When you meet with fire again, your path will be made known to you. And it will not be what you seek but what finds you.*

The cryptic statement carries the weight of true prophecy with it. Aidan grips the spirit's appendage and silently thanks them for their guidance.

"What is your name?"

A smile comes across the spirit's features. A smile that brightens the being's whole countenance.

"*I once had several names, but I have forgotten most of them. The only one I remember is Ashe,*" they say.

"I will remember you, Ashe," Aidan says. He doubts they will meet again.

"*I will remember you, Aidan,*" the spirit says. He doesn't remember saying his name.

The spirit turns and flies away over the sand, a bright flash of light in the air. For a moment Aidan can almost

smell the burning trail left by the spirit, but then the sensation is gone.

"Aidan," Porter calls out. Jogged out of his reverie, Aidan heads across the sand toward his mule. "What did they say?"

"A prophecy," is all Aidan can think to say. He will need to write down the words later and study them to understand. He mounts his mule.

"We should get moving," Porter says.

Far in the distance a storm cloud has formed to their west. Likely it came off the Matraize sea far over the horizon. Though he cannot hear the thunder, he can see the lightning crack across the sky. They turn north again and head toward the Umbrian shield shimmering on the distant horizon.

Twenty-Two

Aidan crossed into Umbra uneventfully. They spent the following night in Jarran's Outpost getting accustomed to the colder weather. A side effect of the shield around the country of Umbra is the colder temperatures retained within. It seemed that the shield guarded a little too well against energy.

By the time they made their trip through the lower towns and into the great cities north, Aidan was wearing his heaviest coat and still shivering through it. Even though the summer had truly come along in the south, Umbra remained in the last legs of a cold spring and would be for another month or so. The first glimpses of Arcta, the Umbrian capital, and the polar cap beyond showed a city dusted with snow, even up to the tall glass spires. The city was not as grand as Cristalspire which they had passed through the day before, but it certainly had the grandeur of a capital.

Their first stop was to the Chulyin residence and meeting his hostess Kensa Chulyin-Siku. He felt fortunate he had met Elise Chulyin at the regional meeting and had at least a minor connection to the family. In his view, staying with them would feel less awkward.

Kensa Chulyin-Siku turned out to be in her forties at most. She stood tall on the porch having heard of their arrival from the butler when Porter rang the door. The butler oversaw the removal of the luggage and the stabling of the mules around the back of the house. The house itself was something of a marvel to Aidan who was accustomed to adobe buildings. This house was constructed of bricks.

The house felt like a cozy place from the outside. The bay windows on either side of the door, the inset panels along the exterior adding detail to the design, the tower to one side that went up another story and no doubt housed someone's study. All of this endeared the place to Aidan. As he stepped across the threshold into the foyer, his eyes feasted on more wood than he had seen in an interior in his whole life. He knew it was common in Umbra to use it in construction even, but he had never in his mind thought it could be decorative as well.

"I see you like our house," Kensa says as she welcomes them in.

"Very much," Aidan answers. "I haven't seen a place like this." He marvels at the large wooden staircase, the wood floor below his feet, and everything else around him.

Kensa smiles at him. "I hate to break your illusion, but half the wood is fake," she says.

"You're kidding," Aidan says. "It can't be! It's too real." Indeed the floorboards below his feet squeaked with every step.

"They are made with resin and stained and polished to resemble wood. It is far more economical," she adds. "We have more wood available up here, what with the eastern forest, but it is too precious to waste everywhere."

Aidan nods in understanding. He continues to look around the foyer, taking in the crystal chandelier up top and every other ornate ornament around him. Even the paintings on the walls held a certain elegance to them.

"Come have some tea," she suggests, leading them into the parlor. "I think after such a long journey a refreshment is necessary."

Porter excuses himself to see about getting Aidan's belongings into his room. Aidan follows Kensa through to the bright room and takes a seat on an extremely comfortable chair. A clock on the wall chimes the hour and he gratefully takes the tea when it is poured for him.

"Tell me about yourself, Aidan," Kensa suggests. "I know all about your studies, but tell me about you, your family, and so on."

Aidan smiles thinking of his family. He talks for almost five minutes straight about his parents, his aunt and uncle, and his cousins, all of whom he left behind in Egraria. Kensa waits patiently, listening to him tell his story and how he got to Umbra.

Then Kensa asks the question, "Were you born a witch?"

Aidan smiles. "It's unusual in a family like mine, but yes, I was born a witch."

"And a writer witch no less," she says. "I'm glad you are here, Aidan. I hope you will be comfortable staying with us."

"It's just you?" Aidan confirms. He knows Kensa is unmarried, but he does not know who else lives in the house.

"Me, my housekeeper, my niece stays sometimes when she is up from university, and of course you met the butler and my valet," she says. "They are here to help if you need anything."

"When will I be going to visit the site?" he asks, referring to the project Kensa has been working on.

"This evening if you are up for it," she says. "I thought we could take a look at the ship structure and you can see the observatory."

"Really? Will they be communicating with Yddril?"

"Of course," Kensa says. "We always communicate with them, every day we can."

A thrill of excitement runs through him as he suddenly can't wait to visit the site. "Can we go sooner?" he asks.

This elicits a laugh from Kensa. "If you are rested enough," she says. "I would suggest seeing your room and getting settled first."

"Yes, but I really want to see this ship you're building. Is it really going to fly to space?" he asks, still not quite believing it.

"We hope so," she answers. "That is what you're here to help with."

"Then we should go visit it."

Porter picks that moment to enter the parlor. He smiles and greets Kensa before saying to Aidan, "I have your things settled in your room. You should check everything before you go anywhere."

"And have you settled yourself in your room?" Kensa asks. "I trust the loft is not too cramped for you."

Porter smiles broadly at her and says, "It's bigger than my room at home."

Kensa nods. "The attic was converted many years ago and makes for a good apartment space." To Aidan she says, "Well, go up and see your room. I'll get myself ready to go to the site and I'll call them over the witchwire to let them know we are coming."

"You have a witchwire here?" he asks.

"Most of Arcta is wired," she explains. "Most of our cities have them in homes."

In Avita Spring, witchwire news was printed in newspapers twice a day. He got spoiled at school in Courtthostur having the witchwire in the common area. To have a communication port at home simply astonished him.

Aidan gets up and heads up the stairs in the direction Porter guides him. Kensa heads into another room and he catches a snippet of her talking to her housekeeper.

Adian's room faces the front street, a good-sized bedroom with an adjoining bathroom. He found his belongings still packed but dusted off and laid out for him on the four-poster bed. A wardrobe, a desk, and a sitting chair all occupy the room. The bay window has a bench and he can see himself sitting there reading or people watching the street below. They are not in the center of town, but the street is a main artery through this neighborhood. He had seen and heard several steam carriages go by on the cobbled street.

Porter begins to help unpack his belongings while Aidan freshens up in the bathroom. It is well appointed with a claw-foot tub and has a door leading into the rear bedroom. That room is unoccupied at the moment.

With Aidan's help, they have his clothes unpacked and the books he insisted on bringing set out on the desk. A wall-mounted shelf above stood empty and waiting for him to arrange his things there. He peers out the window, seeing a horse carriage go by. A few walkers pass the house's gates as well.

Ready for a little adventure, he heads back downstairs. Kensa waits for him in the foyer, pulling on leather gloves with a wool coat buttoned closed. Aidan hugs his coat around himself, Porter doing the same as they prepare to leave. Outside, Kensa's steam carriage waits for them. The three climb in, waiting and the driver turns the carriage down the street.

Aidan had ridden in many carriages before, but he had not been in a steam carriage. It moved faster than he was used to and he gripped the side handle as a reflex to the speed. Kensa assured him he would get used to it. She explained that the bus system switched to steam about a year ago and the whole city was converting. Steam did little to pollute the streets. They also didn't have to worry so much about the horses' needs. They passed a bus on the way to the observatory grounds.

About ten minutes ride from the house, they turned down a winding side street that opened up into the university space. There were two big universities in Arcta, the University of North Umbra and Ridgeview Conservatory. The latter occupied a neighborhood across the city. The campus they pulled into is the University of North Umbra.

Through the university gates, past the walls and to the far end of campus, the space opens up to a large dirt field where the enormous ship sits. The hulking mass looks further along in development than Aidan believed possible. In the sunset light, with the surrounding electric lights coming on, the ship indeed looks meant for the stars.

The ship consisted of two parts. The main part at bottom looked like a long tube space with what are clearly windows on the front end. According to the designs Kensa sent Aidan, this is the part that would launch into space when the time came. It is equipped with two panels meant for capturing solar energy and thus powering the series of electric motors at the rear of the vehicle. On Terra, the thrust would be barely anything against the atmosphere, but in space the story is different. The thrust would be enough to maneuver and with the full use of all motors to travel between Terra and Yddril.

In addition to the electric motors, two solar sails could be deployed to catch the ionic wind from their star Usil. The final diagram sent to Aidan had shown the sails deployed. They could use them even traveling toward the sun if they tacked against the wind the way sailors do in the Falgar. The way back from Yddril would be much simpler.

The second part of the ship is a standard albeit unusually large balloon ship that would take the completed ship to the launch site. Out in the middle of the frozen tundra, a launch tower larger than any building ever constructed reached toward the sky. This skyscraper would drag the ship to its highest point before letting it loose into the atmosphere. A series of chemical rockets would allow the ship to keep going against the force of gravity. The crew would then head into space in a way that had never been done.

As Aidan steps out of the carriage into the shadow of the spaceship, he can't help but stand slack-jawed and head craned back staring at the magnificent structure. Kensa chuckles next to him, no doubt having seen the expression a few times before.

"I see you like our spaceship," she says.

The sunset glow turns the copper-colored metal a golden hue.

"Very much," Aidan answers her. "I would love to ride in it."

Kensa smiles broadly at him. "So would I," she says with passion in her gaze. "The smaller ship at the launch site will be tested in a month, we hope. You should still be here when it goes up."

"That's so exciting."

"Well, come to the observatory. We'll let them wrap up work for the day before I give you the penny tour of the ship," she says.

"Really?"

"Of course! I thought that's what you wanted."

"Yes," Aidan says enthusiastically.

He and Porter follow Kensa around the massive site to a squat building located at the end of the field. The observatory had changed over the years. What started as a ground-based telescope had turned into a radio wave observatory and finally this site that links with the satellite above. Satellites are still relatively new in concept, but a few had been placed in orbit to allow for communication with Yddril. As they head into the observatory control room, he hears for the first time the voices of Yddrilin on the speaker set up at the center of the room.

The words mean nothing to Aidan. He watches though as two observers, one man and one woman, watch over the shoulder of a third young man who scribbles as the message plays. Finally he hands the sheet to the man and sits back in his chair.

"Aidan, this is Myrmen Pender, lead observer tonight," Kensa says, indicating the older gentlemen. "This is Pasca Sambells, our natural philosopher in residence," she says, indicating the woman. "And finally this is Cathal MacGille, a graduate student at North Umbra and scholar of Yddril. Everyone, this is Aidan

Montgomery, one of our borrowed writer witches."

What she didn't say is that Cathal MacGille is clearly a witch. Each of them shake hands with Aidan, but when he gets to Cathal, the witch says, "Writer, huh?"

"Yes," Aidan answers. "And you are a . . . ?"

"Seer," he says. "It comes in handy for the translating."

Aidan had never thought of it that way, but he supposed they could use their abilities to understand languages. The common tongue on Terra is indeed so common that older dialects and languages are slowly dying out. He supposed any proficiency with other languages would be helpful in understanding another planet's language.

"Will you be working with us, Aidan?" Myrmen Pender asks.

"I'm not sure."

Kensa jumps in, "You will be working mostly on the ship, but I think given your enthusiasm we can find some time for you to observe as well."

Aidan nods, understanding. His primary purpose here is to help with the airtight seals on the ship and some of the other miscellaneous engineering tasks. Getting to work in an observatory only sweetened the experience.

"We look forward to having you," Pasca Sembells says with a smile. "We'll be sure to put you to work."

Aidan laughs, understanding that she is teasing.

"For now, I must get my young charge to dinner," Kensa says. "Good to see all of you."

"And we'll see you tomorrow night for your shift," Myrmen Pender adds.

"I haven't forgotten."

With that Kensa ushers them out of the observatory. Aidan regrets leaving, feeling that he could spend days or even weeks in that building studying their neighboring planet. He didn't realize until then just how passionate he was about interplanetary relations. Maybe that would be his calling after all. Maybe the spirit was right.

Kensa leads them back to the steam carriage. The whole ride home he ponders the spirit's words again. *What finds you.* Is this what found him?

He heads into dinner with no more answers than when he left Egraria.

Twenty-Three

After a month of a lull between the two opposing sides in Port Nalrang, the unrest raged in full. The disturbances got to the point that Nadia and Elise were no longer allowed to roam the city even in the limited part of their neighborhood. After a couple days of this, Elise got word that her family was recalling her home to Umbra. With the primary election over and the growing conflict making the city too dangerous, Nadia's parents seized on the opportunity to send her north.

Nadia and Elise had travelled back to Coreton via Avita Spring to pack up their dorm and anything else Nadia would need from home. Then after withdrawing from Fernsby and saying a sentimental farewell to the dean, they set out for Northpass and the Wastewalk. The trip across the Waste was not easy and Nadia regretted missing so many riding lessons. Aside from some soreness they made the trip without incident. So two months after her family called her to Port Nalrang, she finally set foot in Umbra.

The bustling city of Arcta that Elise called home felt busier than any place Nadia had lived except maybe Port Nalrang. And she had not been in Port Nalrang long enough to become accustomed to the city, never mind that the city's unrest had prevented her from exploring much. They immediately made their way to Elise's home where her parents were waiting for them to arrive.

Elise's house in the central part of town was one of many tightly packed, gabled-roof houses that barely have an alley between each other. The cramped spaces aren't appealing to Nadia, but this neighborhood is one of the most sought after in Arcta. The proximity to the Umbrian Royal House and the Parliament District, as well as the downtown area in the other direction, all make the location ideal for anyone working in government. And almost all of Elise's family works in government because of their ties to the Royal Family. The Chulyins are first cousins of the King, Elise's grandmother having been a blood descendent of a Ukiuq. Nadia has always known her friend is of royal blood, but it didn't really sink in what that meant until she set foot into Elise's house.

The first two days in Arcta Nadia spent settling in and getting enrolled at Grandview Academy. It wasn't until later in the week that she finally went to the University of North Umbra campus with Elise to meet with Elise's aunt. That's when she first clamped eyes on Umbra's spaceship. Never in her wildest dreams did she think she would get that close to such a machine, much less would she be a part of the project. But that is exactly what she is going to do. She will help this project go from drawing to space.

It is while working on the project that she and Elise caught up with Aidan again. Kensa had let them know he was staying with her, but they had worked opposite shifts for the most part during the first few days she was there. Then they ran into each other in the hallway and the surprised greeting was enough to tell Nadia they were indeed friends.

At the end of the first week, Kensa decided to host a dinner at her house and bring together the interns and some of the higher ups on the project. This is how Nadia found herself sitting at a dinner table with Aidan on one side and an unknown seer witch on the other side.

"Cathal MacGille," the seer introduces himself.

"Nadia Oswald," she says genially.

"You're the other writer witch," Cathal says. It's not a question.

"Yes," she says. "I take it you're the translator I've heard about?"

He shrugs, clearly too modest to say yes. "I try anyway," he says. "Translating Yddrilin is not easy."

"Do we know what they look like?"

"Yes, but it's not widely known on Terra," he says. "They know what we look like as well. And I'm sure we look as strange to them as they do to us."

Nadia shifts in her seat, uncomfortable in her formal dress. The idea of knowing what the Yddrilin look like is enticing. "Can I see the images the next time I am at the observatory?" she asks.

"I'll have to clear it with Myrmen, but I don't see why not." He pauses before adding in a low voice, "It might disturb you to know."

"It disturbs me more to not know."

"I suppose that's fair."

And they leave the conversation there as Kensa signals it's time to turn. Nadia switches to her other side and smiles at Aidan.

"How have you been?" she asks in a low voice. She

wiggles her eyebrows so he knows she's talking about his anchor witch abilities. She had only just learned the name for it when the conference ended. It shocked her that most people thought there were only three types of witches, not the actual four.

"Managing," he says back in an equally low voice. "My tutor is here in Umbra, so I am getting some help at least."

"The man I met at the meeting?"

"Yes."

"He seemed very genuinely interested in wanting to teach you."

Aidan nods thoughtfully. He glances around the table and so does Nadia. The rest of the group are deep in conversation as the courses change on the table. Only Elise glances her way briefly then goes back to talking to Myrmen Pender who is commanding her complete attention.

Around her she can feel the spell on Aidan flex to include her. It was an odd sensation, as if a slight weight were lifted from her shoulders. "There are only seven anchors that they know of. And it is dangerous for us to spend time together," he says.

"Too obvious?"

"Yes, we are too obvious together. But it's also that we can't really cover the planet when we're clustered," he says.

Nadia nods her head, thinking about the globe back in her classroom in Fernsby and the way the anchors would have to spread out to cover it. "There's not enough, are there?"

"I don't think so," he says. "I wonder if there are more. Or if we only need more now because of Ecrium."

"You mean because of the war."

"Yes," he says. In an even lower voice he says, "It's within our power to stop that kind of thing."

"I had no idea," she says.

"That's why there was a month of relative calm. We did that."

"But there aren't enough of you to help with the war overall."

"No."

Nadia twists her napkin in her lap. "We have to talk about this in private again."

"We'll find a way," he says quickly. "I'll pay a call on you and Elise if necessary."

Then the next course is before them and there is no time for talking.

Some two hours later, Nadia and Elise sit in the back of a steam carriage riding to Elise's home. They are alone and Elise finally asks, "What were you and Aidan talking about? You seemed very engrossed."

"His power," she says. She tries to explain but realizes the spell is still affecting her. The words "anchor witch" die in her throat. She tries a different tactic. "Are you sure you want to know a deadly secret?"

Elise looks at her seriously. Her friend knows she wouldn't ask if it weren't important. And while Nadia is sure Elise can be trusted with Aidan's secret, she doesn't know if Elise wants to know what his secret is.

"You can tell me," she says. "I'll take it to my grave."

Nadia nods. She puts a hand on her throat and concentrates for a moment. She remembered seeing the spell at the meeting and again at dinner. Like a vague outline of light in the air around Aidan. But in that spell, she could see the key to it. Goliyant had told her not every writer witch could do that and only a very few could see spells like she could. She had never had the opportunity until she met Aidan.

With some difficulty, she uses the key to unravel the binding on her throat. And then she feels the weight lift again, the feeling of freeing from the spell.

"No one knows what I'm about to tell you. Or no humans and only a handful of witches," she says. "I learned about it at the conference in Courtthostur."

Elise's eyebrows go up, perhaps at how long her friend had kept the secret.

"There are not three classifications of witches. There are four," she says. "I am not the rarest kind, Aidan is."

"What is the fourth classification?"

"Anchor witch," Nadia says, her voice cracking over the words. "Aidan has a spell around himself keeping people from saying those words."

"Anchor witch."

"Yes. I didn't understand at first either."

"Hm. I wonder though."

"What do you mean?"

"Well," she says, "Wilhelm Martinsson is an anchor then, isn't he?"

Nadia nods, remembering the man.

"It was so comforting to be around him, I remember thinking he reminded me of my father," she says. "I couldn't explain it at the time."

"Aidan doesn't feel like that," Nadia says

thoughtfully. "Maybe because he's not well-practiced yet?"

"Maybe."

The steam carriage pulls up to Elise's house. The two of them hop out and head inside. The housekeeper greets them as they head up the stairs to their rooms. They both head into Elise's room and she shuts the door behind them.

"Why is it kept secret?"

"I think for the same reasons I became a writer witch."

Elise blinks at the answer. "You mean someone might try to kill him for his abilities."

"I think someone already tried, given the spell."

A dark shadow passes over Elise's face. "Like how someone might try to kill you for it."

Nadia's stomach flips. She had always thought of her power as a burden, as something to be hidden from her family, as something she didn't fully understand. She never thought of it as a threat to her other than if her mother found out. It had never occurred to her that she could be the one to wind up with a knife in her chest.

Nadia sits down on Elise's bed.

Elise sits next to her and squeezes her hand. "I wish

I could help with what you're feeling," she says. "But I'm glad you're here and you're protected in Umbra at least."

"I wonder for how long."

And the truth is she couldn't know how long she would escape conscription in Umbra. Eventually she would be called up. Eventually she would need to return to Egraria.

A knock on the door draws her out of her reverie. The housekeeper pokes her head in and smiles.

"Tomorrow's problem," Elise says. "We should go to bed."

"I think that's a good idea."

Nadia gets up to head out of Elise's room.

"Goodnight," Elise says.

Nadia echoes the sentiment feeling the night will be anything but good. She heads to her room.

Twenty-Four

A month into Aidan's internship, Kensa decided it was time to try to airproof the ship. They had finally perfected the equations necessary for the spell to run accurately. The ship had been sealed. The final parts had been installed. It was now only a matter of gathering the right people together and preparing the engineering spells accordingly.

Several elementals who had been working on the project off and on all came to campus at the same time. The air crackled with energy as they circled each other, the bulk of them being water and air elements. After a week one more elemental showed up who Aidan recognized. Grappley would be their fire elemental on the project.

"It's good to see you again," Aidan had greeted him

when he arrived.

The elemental had seemed surprised by the genial greeting. However he had responded in a friendly way and said he was only there long enough to work on the project. He had been conscripted into the Egrarian army.

The news from the south had gotten more and more grave as the weeks rolled on. He had spoken to Nadia about their mutual conscription concerns no more than a few days before Egraria started calling people up. For them, going home would likely mean getting called. They could even be called from Umbra and compelled to return to Egrarian soil. The thought unsettled them both.

As the group gathered in the north, the south experienced more and more turmoil. Another series of bombings in Port Nalrang made Aidan fear for Howells's safety. He thought the anchor could take care of himself, but he still worried about him. Either way he was so far from Port Nalrang that there was nothing he could do.

So as the week finally arrived for them to airproof the ship, Aidan found himself in a group of seven magicals and one human. Three elementals, four witches, and Elise were all there to oversee the work. As competent as Nadia seemed at mathematics, Elise was by far the genius. She had run through most of their calculations and made minor corrections here and there to help get everything in place. She was attending the spellcasting to make sure nothing went awry with that part of things.

Besides Grappley, the two air elementals and water elemental all seemed chummy enough. Nadia appeared to know the water elemental and called him by his former name rather than his elemental name, Hydris. A caster witch they had all met during their time working would be joining them to facilitate the activation of the spell. Cathal would be their seer witch and would monitor everything about the spell.

On a clear afternoon day without any wind, the seven of them stood under the main part of the ship, waiting for instructions to start. The rest of the team monitoring their work remained huddled in the observatory room, peering through a large window. Kensa is among those watching.

Each of them has a small radio wave communicator through which Kensa began calling the sequence of events.

"Cathal, be at the ready and feel free to interrupt if needed."

"Yes, ma'am."

"Sebastian," she says to the caster witch, "you may activate the spell. The rest of you be ready to activate your parts."

Aidan's stomach churns nervously. He can't help but feel on the precipice of something big and momentous. He takes a steadying breath.

Sebastian begins.

The feeling of magic rising around them threatens to choke Aidan's breathing. Sebastian is a powerful caster witch. Aidan exchanges a nervous look with Nadia who also seems to be struggling. Neither of them had ever been part of such a powerful casting before.

Just as the spell feels on the brink of breaking, as the energy rises to a point that is almost unbearable, Cathal nods at Aidan and Nadia, guiding the casting process. With another exchanged glance, Aidan and Nadia both tap into their powers.

Their powers are not dissimilar, but with Aidan an anchor posing as a writer, he is careful not to draw from his full scope of magic. Instead he follows Nadia's lead and matches her power for power. The feeling of choking subsides completely as his power stands up to Sebastian's mighty caster power.

Through his power he can feel every curve and joint

of the ship. Sebastian did a great job of taking hold of it. Now Aidan and Nadia are feeding the spell and guiding it through the calculations that airproof the ship. He finds himself taking her hand and working closer in tandem, making the magic easier to enact. They wrap the ship in line after line of power, a faint glow in the air around the ship the only tell of their work. When they have enough lines matching the ship's curves, they hold the spell in place and wait for the elementals.

The two air elementals start. Their magic is incomprehensible to Aidan. It feels like a summer breeze and a winter blizzard all at once. Again Aidan feels like the power is choking him, but this is different. Almost like he is being smothered. The feeling only deepens when Hydris joins them. Then it goes from feeling like a breeze to feeling like a dense fog around them. And this is the moment the elementals' powers become visible. Thin, intricate lattice lines of air-contained water surround the ship in a tidy net.

Aidan's jaw drops at the sheer control the three of them have. He had seen nothing like it before. As their focus shifts to containing the elements themselves, he feels the smothering sensation ease up some. He is able to just watch in amazement as the air and water begin to rotate around the ship. The elements are seeking weaknesses in the spell woven by the witches. They are collectively teaching the metal of the ship to act as a barrier against them. The only thing left is to add Grappley's fire to the mix and then tie the whole spell together.

As the fire elemental begins his work, thin lines of flames begin to sprout in the air around them. For a moment Aidan's heart races fearing the worst, but the lines are so thin and so controlled he cannot fathom the power to contain it. Until Grappley moves his power into the spell as well. Then the smothering sensation disappears completely and is replaced with a crackling, burning feeling like a mild sunburn. He glances at Nadia and sees her face is flushed from the heat. The other witches' faces are the same and the air and water elementals too seem to be struggling. Aidan reaches up and touches his cheek to find it cool to the touch. The fire clearly isn't bothering him as much as the others.

Several minutes pass as Grappley carefully weaves his fire in between and around the other elements around the ship. The intricate net became downright complicated to the point it looked more like a woven tapestry than a net. As Aidan watches, Grappley's skin takes on a slight glow from the fire. In that moment he feels a sense of awe, but he is immediately distracted by a sudden flair of power.

Nadia takes in a sharp breath next to him. Her hand in his squeezes for a moment in anxiety. Aidan looks up.

The fire has taken over the net. Their power beneath it struggled to hold the element back. Grappley is losing control.

The water vaporizes and the air only feeds the fire. If Grappley can't get control of the fire, the spell might break and thus take the ship with it.

"Grappley!" they hear through the communicator. "Pull the fire back!"

The panic in Kensa's voice is enough to make Aidan's heart race. He realizes the group of them, including Elise standing some five feet behind, are all in danger if the fire gets out of control.

Grappley must have realized the same thing. He steps forward and raises one hand to the fire.

The fire dives toward him.

Grappley's skin glows brighter, drowning out the human qualities all elementals have. Then Aidan realizes where his sense of deja vu comes from. Ashe. The fire spirit he met a month ago in the Waste. They looked like that. They had glowing skin that wasn't really skin.

Aidan lets go of Nadia's hand. She looks at him in concern as he rushes to Grappley's side. He needs to warn him. If he doesn't get control, he could become a spirit.

"Grappley! You have to stop!"

The fire elemental doesn't seem to hear him.

"Grappley!"

Aidan reaches for his free hand. A garbled message in the communicator speaks a warning too late. He grabs Grappley's hand.

Immediately he knows his mistake. The fire leaps for Aidan as well and surrounds his arms. He uses every ounce of power in his possession to help control the heat. He doesn't have enough. His skin begins to burn.

"Aidan!" several voices call out behind him.

Then something comes loose inside Grappley. Aidan doesn't know how he feels it in the face of the pain. He doesn't know why the pain suddenly subsides to nothing and his skin begins to cool. He doesn't know why the fire dances playfully around his skin. He only knows he needs to stop the fire from burning the ship.

So he stops the fire.

He feels a hand on his shoulder as he passes out.

Twenty-Five

Nadia knows she made a mistake.

This time she knows it because she felt this sensation before.

Aidan's anchor power comes loose from him and dives into Nadia. She feels the war begin within her. The writer power and the anchor power battle for control over abilities. She can't control the scream.

"Stay back!" she screams at the witches who crowd her. "Don't touch me!"

She knows if they do the writer witch power will take over them. They will feel the same kind of pain she is currently wracked with. This pain did not happen when she held the hand of the writer witch. But she was human then. She had no power to conflict with then.

Aidan's unconscious body is next to her where she

kneels doubled over in pain in the dirt. Grappley's glowing form is just past Aidan. The new spirit seems confused and unsure what to do. But the fire has stopped now. At least the fire in the air. The fire within was just beginning for both Aidan and her.

Elise closes the distance between them. Nadia realizes what she is feeling and looks with terrified eyes at her friend. She looks down at the hand holding hers.

"No!"

Too late.

The writer witch power, her familiar power that she had learned to live with, suddenly vacates her. Immediately the pain eases.

Elise's eyes go wide and her hand goes to her heart in shock.

"What's happening?"

"Elise isn't human anymore," Cathal says matter-of-factly.

Tears stream down Elise's face. Nadia embraces her best friend. The two of them sob on each other's shoulders.

The group from the observatory room has joined them under the shadow of the ship. Nadia is aware of the bustling activity around them, but she can't pay attention to it. The anchor power settles into her chest like a heavy steadying weight. She feels herself again in a way she hasn't in a long time. She feels certainty and confidence surging through her. The relief it brings only makes the tears come stronger.

"Elise, Nadia," Kensa says softly. "We need to get you two home."

The other elementals help them to their feet. Hydris has picked up the still-unconscious Aidan.

"Is he going to be alright?" Nadia asks softly.

"He will be," Hydris says with sympathy in his eyes. "So will you."

Nadia nods. "Thanks, Adriel," she says. She is the only one to use his former name. Now she wonders what Aidan will be called. She wonders what Aidan's life will be like now that he is no longer a witch.

Nadia looks down at herself. Like on that day years ago when she held the dying witch's hand, her skirts are covered with dirt. A layer of ash covers her hands from where she touched Aidan. She is a disaster again only this time her mother isn't here to see it.

Elise leans on her, still shocked by the new power within her. She hugs her friend, knowing the turmoil within.

"It looks like Aidan's writer power passed into Nadia and displaced hers into Elise," Cathal says. "It looks like Aidan's power was stronger."

The assessment is fair if not accurate. It was the anchor power that displaced it. She somehow doubted her writer power would have left her. She somehow doubted she would have ended up with Aidan's power if he were in fact a writer.

"Come inside and wait for the carriage there," Kensa says. The concern in her voice isn't just for her niece but for Nadia as well. A hint of guilt flits across her features when Nadia looks up at her.

The girls walk gingerly together toward the observatory. Once inside they find themselves wrapped in blankets and served cold tea and given damp towels to wipe their faces off. Some fifteen minutes pass before the steam carriage from Elise's home arrives. Elise's mother is waiting for them.

"Are you two alright?" she asks them both. To Kensa she asks, "What happened?"

"A transfer of powers. Elise is a writer witch now," Kensa says.

"How?"

"We can discuss all the details later. They should get

home."

"Of course," Elise's mother says. "Are you two alright?" she repeats her question.

Nadia nods, not having words for what's happening inside her.

"I'm tired," Elise says weakly. "I just want to take a nap."

Nadia remembers needing to sleep after gaining her power. As if she needed to reset herself somehow and sleep was the only way to do so.

"Come, we'll go home. You can take all the time you need."

The carriage ride home is silent and uneventful. Elise's mother keeps sneaking looks at the two of them in a worried way. She is vastly different from Nadia's mother who would be berating her at this moment. Worse she might have disowned her if she knew she was a witch.

As if reading her mind, Elise's mother suddenly says, "You don't want your mother to know what happened, I take it."

"No," Nadia says bluntly. "She'll kill me."

Concern and anger flit through Elise's mother's eyes. "It will be our secret."

Relief floods Nadia.

"What's going to happen to Aidan?"

The best she can say is, "He's an elemental now."

Elise leans into Nadia's shoulder and rests her head there. "I'm sorry I didn't listen."

"Don't be sorry," Nadia says as the carriage pulls up to the house. "You can put your math genius to work now."

Elise laughs weakly and even her mother smiles.

They climb out of the carriage and the two girls immediately head upstairs. Nadia goes to her room and washes the ash off her hands and face. She then changes out of her dress and into a light afternoon dress, wiping down her legs and arms between outfits. She is about to lay down on the bed but makes another decision. Nadia goes and knocks on Elise's door.

"Come in," the soft voice says.

Elise is sitting still covered in dirt on her bed.

Nadia shuts the door behind her. Without asking and without needing to be told, she begins to clean Elise's hands and face from all the dirt and ash that are there.

When she has wiped the last of the ash from Elise's cheeks, she says, "You should change."

Elise just nods.

Nadia pulls out one of Elise's soft, white dresses she prefers in the afternoon. In the kind way only a close friend could do, she helps Elise out of her walking dress and into the afternoon dress. She takes the time to wipe down Elise's arms and legs from the same dirt that was on Nadia.

A rap on the door signals the arrival of Elise's mother and the housekeeper. They bring tea which Nadia is relieved to find is chamomile.

"Go ahead and nap. We'll see you downstairs for dinner later," Elise's mother says. She kisses her daughter on the cheek and murmurs love to her. Then she gives Nadia a hug and says, "I know you've been through it today. But I'm glad you were there for my daughter."

The kind words catch her so off-guard Nadia can only nod.

The two of them leave the room and softly shut the door as Nadia and Elise both lay down on Elise's bed.

After about ten minutes of silence, Elise whispers, "I'm scared."

Nadia wraps her arms around her best friend and says, "Me too."

Elise cries quiet sobs until she falls asleep. Nadia is not far behind her.

The light has shifted by the time she awakens. Nadia can already tell it is evening outside. On this day that felt like so many unexpected changes, a sinking feeling settles into her stomach. Suddenly she feels like this day isn't over yet.

Elise is gone from the bed, presumably having woken sometime earlier. The battle between the powers inside her had taken it out of Nadia. It didn't surprise her that she slept for a long time. She gets up and goes to the door. The moment she opens it that sinking feeling only deepens.

Low voices from below murmur words she can only half make out. The one sentence she can hear is, "Well we have to tell her."

She freezes at the top of the stairs. That bad feeling creeping over her overwhelms suddenly. She swallows and slowly makes her way down the steps. At the bottom of the stairs, she hears the voices more clearly but they stop when she hits a creaky step. She heads into the parlor. There she finds Elise and her parents and the housekeeper all waiting with Kensa. In Kensa's hand is a witchwire note.

"What is it?" Nadia asks.

"You should sit down," Elise's mother says.

Elise doesn't wait for Nadia to move. She just goes to her friend and takes her hand.

"What's going on?" Nadia asks. Her nervousness is rising. Elise guides her to a couch and they sit down together.

Elise's mother kneels down in front of her and takes Nadia's free hand. "We just received word from your family," she says. There is a pause. The tension in the room is palpable. "I'm afraid your mother had a heart attack. They took her to the hospital but there was nothing that could be done."

"What?"

"I'm afraid she died," Elise's mother says.

A thousand different emotions ranging from relief to anger to grief. Overwhelmed she bursts into tears. Elise throws her arms around her and she finds herself crying in the arms of her best friend.

Her mother died. She doesn't know what to feel. She just knows she is no longer in danger from her own family. At least she thinks she isn't. And then a thought occurs to her.

After a long time of crying into Elise's arms, she steadies herself. She wipes her eyes with the handkerchief someone handed her and asks, "I have to go back, don't I?"

"I'm afraid so," Elise's mother says. The Chulyin's haven't left the room. They waited out Nadia's crying and didn't shy away from the tough emotions. She looks around at them.

"Can Elise come with me?"

"Of course," Elise says, not waiting for her parents to say anything. They would not have objected. Each of them is nodding or giving their assent.

"Do you want any dinner? Or would you like to just go back to bed?"

Nadia's stomach rumbles. The energy toll of witchcraft had finally caught up to her. She feels hollow inside. "I think some dinner then bed."

"Would you like a tray in your room?"

"Yes, please."

"I'll take her up," Elise says. She immediately stands up and helps Nadia to her feet. Together they make their way to the stairs and back the way Nadia came less than an hour ago. Elise guides Nadia to her bedroom and pours a glass of water from the bedside pitcher. She contemplates for a moment and then concentrates. A moment later the glass has a layer of condensation. It's cold to the touch when Nadia takes it from her.

"Thank you."

"I'm here for you."

"I know," Nadia says. "I don't know what to feel."

"That's ok," Elise says, squeezing Nadia's free hand. "We'll get you to Port Nalrang and go from there."

Nadia sets the glass down and hugs her friend again. "Thank you for being my friend."

"Thank you for being mine."

The housekeeper brings up dinner, a light soup that Nadia eats slowly. Then she lays back down and it's Elise's turn to comfort her during this day of ups and downs.

Thinking back to this morning she could not have anticipated any of what just occurred.

Part of her is glad she isn't a skilled seer.

Part of her wishes she could have seen all of this coming.

Twenty-Six

Aidan sleeps for three days.

When he wakes the first thing, he notices is the lack of the binding spell around him. No doubt the spell collapsed when he lost his anchor witch powers. He looks around the infirmary, probably the university infirmary, and wonders what it means to be an elemental. He studies his hand and tries to call any of his spells. None of them come to him. He is definitely no longer a witch.

A nurse comes into the empty infirmary and sees he's awake. She comes over to him and places a damp towel on his forehead. The towel feels odd, like it's incongruent for him to feel something cooling.

"How are you feeling?"

"A little groggy," he says.

"You're running a fever, but that might be normal for elementals," she says. "We're trying to find out."

"How are the others?" he asks.

"Grappley has moved on. He stayed long enough to help get you settled, but he has since left for the Waste," she explained.

"What about Nadia? And Elise?"

"They are doing fine. Both are writer witches," a fact Aidan knows is false but he keeps quiet. "However, they have left Umbra for Egraria."

Aidan blinks. It makes no sense. "What? Why?"

"Miss Oswald's mother died of a heart attack. They are going for the funeral and other arrangements."

A sense of sadness comes over Aidan. He knows Nadia did not have a good relationship with her mother, but that doesn't change the fact that death is sad. "I'm sorry for her," he says. "I wish I could help."

"Heal," the nurse says. "Then you can figure out what you can do to support her."

"Will I go home?" he asks. "Are they sending me back?"

"It's likely, yes. Your family's man, Porter I think, has been checking in with the doctors every day," she adds. "He will likely be by later. I'm sure he will tell you the plans."

"Thank you," Aidan says.

A wave of exhaustion comes over him again. The nurse seems to sense this. She removes the cloth from his forehead and checks his temperature. She makes him drink a little water, though the fluid tastes strange to him now.

"Get some rest," she says. "I'll let the doctors know you woke. The next time you wake up one of them will be here."

Aidan nods. He closes his eyes and barely a minute later is fast asleep again.

The next time Aidan wakes there is a doctor in the ward. Next to the doctor is a witch healer and the two of them are deep in conversation. When they see Aidan is awake, they take seats on either side of his bed.

"How are you feeling?"

Aidan shrugs. He doesn't know how to answer that question. People really need to stop asking him. Other than feeling like something is missing, he doesn't know how to feel about anything else. And the something that is missing—his witchcraft—would not be coming back anytime soon.

"I don't know," he says.

"Any pain? Any discomfort?"

"Not really. Just tired."

"That's too be expected, given the amount of energy that passed through you," the doctor says. "This is Magnus Brink. He's a healer who has some familiarity with elementals, albeit with air elementals."

Aidan shakes the healer's hand. The warmth of witch magic simmered below the surface of the healer. But for the first time he meets the power not with recognition but with difference. He feels different from the witch. And part of him almost feels relaxed.

"Could you give us a moment?" Magnus says to the doctor and the nurse. The pair of them step away and head down the infirmary ward to sit out of earshot.

"My power doesn't recognize yours," Aidan says.

"You will have to get used to that, I'm afraid." He pauses, glances at the doctor and nurse who are consulting on something, and then plunges forward. In a low voice he says, "Can I ask if you were an anchor witch?"

Aidan blinks at the question. It never occurred to him that someone would just figure it out. And now that he no longer is an anchor, the idea of hiding it feels strange.

"I was," he says.

"The others have bought the explanation that you were a stronger witch than Miss Oswald, but I suspected the truth."

"Yes," Aidan says. "I'm not sure how it would work if we were both writer witches."

"Miss Chulyin would probably still have become a witch," Magnus says. "The power would simply have sought a void."

"So no matter what, things would have changed," he says. He looks at his hand and feels the heat under his skin. He feels the fire ready to come when he calls.

"Yes, things would have changed."

"I don't understand what I am now."

There is a part of Aidan that feels completely lost, so totally unanchored, it makes his previous incarnation as an anchor witch so laughable. His lack of stability before only feels worse now. But another part of him feels more like himself now that he isn't fighting his power. The chaotic nature of fire means he isn't feeling like he's fighting a stable influence. His own chaotic spirit feels relaxed.

"Do you need anything?" Magnus asks.

"I don't think so." He pauses. "When can I leave?"

"I think another day or so. You have to go back to Egraria," Magnus says.

"I think I expected that."

"What you don't know is that Egraria joined the war effort with Rebluinia," Magnus says with a concerned look.

A grim look of dawning comes over Aidan's face. "And I will be conscripted if I haven't already."

Magnus reaches into his coat pocket and pulls out a thin, folded piece of paper. "They conscripted you the day the transition was made known to them."

Aidan sighs. "I guess it is inevitable."

"Not necessarily," Magnus says. "You can always seek asylum here."

The surprise Aidan feels makes him consider the idea. But he dismisses it almost immediately. While he does feel he will be used by Egraria, he also feels like he can't leave the country without seeing his family and explaining to them what happened. And he worries about retaliation against his family if he doesn't go back. He can't do that to them.

Aidan shakes his head. "I can't. I have too much family there."

Magnus gives a wan half-smile. "Well, if you ever

need a place to seek refuge, remember the option."

"I will."

"Get some rest."

Magnus pats Aidan's forearm. The man's touch feels almost cold to him.

The healer gets up and heads across the infirmary saying, "Don't burn the place down."

Aidan snorts. The funny thing is he doesn't know how.

A few minutes later the nurse comes with a pile of letters and notes for him. She also brings a glass of water which he drinks reluctantly. The water tastes terrible now. She looks at him sympathetically but explains he must keep his human self still functioning. She leaves him to rest some more.

Aidan goes through the letters and notes, finding a lot of random messages from all over Umbra and some from Egraria asking for his assistance on various projects. He is immediately overwhelmed by the interest and wants nothing more than to run away and spend the rest of his life roaming the Waste. He suddenly understands why so many fire elementals and fire spirits live in the Waste as free roaming hermits.

At the bottom of the pile, two handwritten notes

stand out from the typecast ones. The two notes are from Nadia and Elise. They both left him messages before leaving for Egraria. Elise's note simply wishes for his speedy recovery and lets him know she is doing well and settling into her new power. The note is kind and Aidan feels touched that she left him one.

Nadia's note is more serious in tone and talks broadly about her power. One paragraph in particular stands out.

It reads:

> *I know you might be trying to understand and settle into your new abilities. I know how that feels and how you must be struggling. But now that things are "as they are" I feel that things are as they are meant to be. I feel like you and I and Elise are exactly as we all should be. We have each taken a strange path to get here. We have each stumbled along the way. But I think now we are where we must be. And now we can move forward and find the paths we were meant to be on all along.*

The words "as they are" tell Aidan she is talking about the anchor witch power. His power. And of course she would know how it is to have a new power within. She got her writer witch power that way. It occurs to Aidan then that she has gotten a power twice now. She has been three different versions of herself and yet she is the same.

Maybe Nadia is right. Maybe they really are all where they need to be.

He sets the letters on the side table, feeling himself drifting off again. Though it is still light outside, he knows he can sleep some more.

His last thoughts are of the Waste and how alluring that wide expanse of emptiness feels now. He wonders how long it will be before he joins the other hermits in the desert.

Twenty-Seven

"You will help them."

Nadia grinds her teeth as her father repeats himself again. She feels her power flaring inside of her, feeling her power holding her steady in the face of her anger.

"No, I won't help a war that will result in so many people dead," she repeats. She is still young enough that she knows her protest will go unheard.

He ignores her words.

In the three weeks since her mother's funeral, she has found herself in an argument with her father time and time again. She was right all these years. She was right about him knowing about her witch power. She was so right she regrets it.

The conscription came for Nadia within two weeks of her mother's death. She stared at the letter dumbfounded that they had her on their register. Then again Umbra had her on their register so she shouldn't be surprised. Appalled maybe, but not surprised.

Her father's reaction only deepens her regret. He sees her as an opportunity to pull in the base. To pull in the voters and help him win over the witches as well. He had to change his messaging and somewhat blame his past beliefs on her mother. It is working though. He is gaining in popularity. And he sees her responding to the conscription call as a patriotic act that could win him more votes.

But Nadia is a pacifist. She figured that out during her first confrontation at Fernsby. The bullies there, namely Nessie Lamont, didn't find her very fun to pick on. She just didn't react to them. She didn't give them anything to enjoy.

She thinks her pacifism comes from watching the writer witch die. He never had a chance and she wishes he did. Even though she wouldn't be a witch now, she still wishes the altercation never happened. No one should die like that.

Nadia waits for her father to say more, but he doesn't. She knows it's pointless to argue with him or with the Conscription Authority. Neither listen to reason. They all just feel that witches must do their part. Witches make up less than half of the population. Many believe that witches owe the population some of their power. But witches are just people. And no person should owe anyone for the space they take up.

She finally excuses herself and leaves the parlor, the views over the city again playing havoc with her need to be outside. She feels steady now, though. Steady in herself and less restless. For the first time in a long time, she knows who she is and what she can do. The anchor power settles in more snugly every day. And like she told Aidan, she feels the power is where it should be.

Elise is in their shared bedroom when she comes in. The second bed Elise uses is up against the wall, but she doesn't mind. Elise sits at Nadia's desk writing something. She looks up and closes her fountain pen when Nadia comes in.

"How did it go?" she asks softly.

"About as expected," Nadia answers with a shrug. "He won't budge."

"You once again need the help of witches but can't get their help."

"Tell me about it."

Nadia flops down on her bed. The bed sits with the

headboard up against the wall and she lays down exactly on the end of it where it sits under the middle of the room. The design painted on the ceiling is that of a sky with angels in the corners. She always found the design peculiar and a little unsettling. Angels are ancient folklore now, but some people believe they existed. Some people believe they still exist and are a kind of spirit. Nadia doesn't believe that. Or else they too would have been exploited like so many species are.

"Have you heard from Aidan?"

Nadia sits up on the edge of the bed. "He sent a witchwire saying he was doing well. He will be in Port Nalrang next week," she says. She pulls the witchwire message out of her pocket and hands it to Elise. The message is time stamped from three days ago. There must have been a delay getting it out of Umbra.

"Will he show you to the person when he is here?"

"I will make sure it happens."

The determination in Nadia's eyes makes her friend sit up a little straighter. Nadia doesn't even realize she is doing it, but when her emotions flair up, the anchor power makes everyone around her feel a little more themselves. Elise had told her. Sometimes Nadia wonders how Aidan kept it secret for so long.

Nadia lets out a dramatic sigh. "Will you go with me to the Conscription Authority?"

"Now?"

"Yes, I have to report by half past four or they'll come find me."

"Of course," Elise says. She turns back to her papers and opens her pen again. "I'll finish this work for my aunt and we can send it while we're out."

Nadia smiles fondly at her best friend. "I told you you'd make a good writer witch."

Elise snorts. "I'm certainly learning it," she says. There is a pause as Elise looks up and studies her friend. "You make a good anchor too."

"You think so?" Nadia feels like she is understanding her power better, but the outside confirmation is still helpful.

"I think so."

Elise puts her pen away and fans her pages to help them dry more quickly. The fountain pens dry quickly enough though so she is done in a moment. She folds up the pages and puts them in an envelope that is pre-marked with a witchwire address and the official Umbrian seal. The characteristic polar cap and Arcta skyline make up the middle, standing out on the beige paper. Then

Elise is done and she gets up from Nadia's desk.

"Ready."

Nadia extracts herself from her bed and goes to put on a hat and coat. It is not cold outside, but the city is windy. They would not be going far but she still needed something to keep the wind out. Elise similarly dons a hat and coat, checking her clothing quickly in the floor length mirror. They head out of her bedroom, softly closing the door behind her.

Her father is in his study now, working on some legal documents or other. He looks up when Nadia pokes her head in and nods cordially at Elise.

"Finally going to do your duty?" he says.

Resenting the tone, she nonetheless answers, "Yes."

Her father reaches for a sealed envelope and holds it out for her. She crosses the thick carpet of his study to take it from him. Her father is framed by the city buildings in the windows behind him. It leaves his face in shadow while the rest of the room is brightly lit. Nadia takes the envelope, feeling the heavy sheaf of several pages within.

"Would you be kind enough to take that to the witchwire and have it sent to the address there? Let me give you the money for it," he adds, reaching into a desk drawer for a parcel jingling with coins. He hands her two silver deniers for the mailing and a gold denier as well.

"What's this for?"

"For you and Elise to go shopping," he says. "I've asked Kaye to accompany you to keep you safe. But you haven't had any clothes in ages and it's time you look the part of a working witch."

Surprise crosses Nadia's face. Her father is correct. She has outgrown her clothes as is made obvious by the ankle of her boot showing below her skirts. And he is also correct in saying she does not have the proper attire for a working witch.

"I am barely fourteen."

"Yes, but you do work."

She concedes that fact.

"Had we talked about this sooner, I would have had this rectified immediately. You need the utilitarian clothing of a working witch," he says. "And you also need the attire of a high stature witch. Both can be solved in one trip." He looks at Elise behind her. "I assume your family won't object to you doing some shopping?"

Elise smiles genially. "Of course not. I'm sure they take a similar view of wardrobe, Mr. Oswald."

Her father smiles at Elise. She so rarely sees him smile that Nadia is taken aback by it. He has smiled at her a few times and they were good moments indeed. He is just too serious of a man to smile much.

He says to both of them, "Well, take the time you need. It is half past one. I trust you'll be home in time for dinner, with some clothing on the way behind you."

Nadia couldn't help but think he makes shopping sound like a chore. Still. He is correct in this and she does wish to have clothing she isn't afraid of messing up while working.

"See you at dinner, father," she says.

He acknowledges the comment then goes back to his work. If there's one thing Nadia knows, it's that she doesn't wish to be a lawyer. The work is too intensive for her.

They head out the door with Kaye in tow. In the lift ride down to the ground floor, she can't help but think she is going to meet her future. She can't help but think that this is both a beginning and an ending of something. She just can't figure out what.

Twenty-Eight

A week into training with the Conscription Authority, Nadia is grateful to her father for providing the wardrobe needed to be a working witch. The women's trousers are a far cry from what her mother's standards would allow, but she found them infinitely more comfortable and useful. She wore them tucked into her boots and belted with a small pouch for spellcasting supplies on the waist. With that she wears a heavy linen shirt and a utilitarian jacket with a half dozen pockets. She is able to easily roll up her sleeves to free her hands and wrists to work.

Nadia is doing just that as she stands in the middle of the proving grounds outside of Port Nalrang's city limits. The day is windy as usual. She wears amber-tinted goggles and a mask over her nose and mouth to keep the sand off her face. The pins holding her hat in place are being tested in the extreme. She would be freezing if not for the warmth her magic provides.

Elise sometimes accompanies her to these training sessions. Sometimes she even joins in to practice her arts. Neither of them is skilled yet, but they are both willing. Her Conscription Authority liaison finds their willingness a bigger asset than their power. He is always saying that wanting to learn is better than having the power and being unwilling.

"Well done, Miss Oswald," her liaison says. Arnaldo Sala stands at five feet seven but feels taller because of how he carries himself. His dark discerning eyes reveal a sharpness of mind that Nadia has come to trust and respect. His patience with her ignorance has been never-ending.

"Thank you, Mr. Sala," she says, turning to him as he approaches with Elise in tow. Both of them are wearing goggles and cloth masks as well.

"I would like you and Miss Chulyin to work together on the next one," he says. He gestures across the proving ground. The dusty field stands empty of any object for the time being. Sometimes they put a large container or an old broken-down steam carriage out there and ask the conscripts to move it or otherwise manipulate it. Today they are working with water and wind. Today he is asking her to write the spell from scratch and call down a rain shower.

Elise nods enthusiastically at being asked to join in. She studied the weather far more diligently at Fernsby than Nadia ever did. Maybe she can understand it well enough to help weave an effective spell.

"I want you to make it rain. And make it rain significantly enough that we have a muddy field for a week," he says decisively.

Sala leaves them in the field and returns to the edges of the proving grounds, standing far enough away that he would not get hit with any of the rain. Presumably anyway. Nadia thinks she might have to test that theory.

Elise stands next to Nadia and slips her hand into Nadia's. A jolt of power and emotion runs through Nadia, her stomach flipping at the contact. She squeezes her best friend's hand and they look at each other and nod.

"Ready?"

"Ready."

"You know what to do?" Nadia asks.

Elise nods. She had been watching from the sidelines the whole morning. Nadia wondered how interesting it must have been to watch Nadia barely produce a misty rain. Never mind that now though. They had work to do.

Nadia lifts her left hand and Elise lifts her right. They both call up their power from within themselves. Nadia recognizes the feel of Elise's power as she had worked with Aidan a few times. The touch of the former writer's power felt familiar in a way that made it easy to work with. Every time she and Elise had connected to try even the smallest thing, she noted that familiarity and reveled in it. Somehow the familiar power coming from her best friend felt right.

Together they work to call rain in the desert. They work to lift the small amount of moisture in the air up to a point in the atmosphere where it will condense and form a cloud. Then it is a matter of keeping the moisture together long enough to actually rain out of the cloud. They push the microdroplets up and down and up and down in the atmosphere. Wind whips around them as they force the droplets up and down. Slowly they coalesce and grow, forming larger and larger drops that eventually fight to stay in the air.

Above them the cloud they formed turns darker and more menacing. It is not a thunderstorm, but it will rain heavily on the field when they finally let it go.

"Ready?" Nadia asks, her voice raised above the wind.

Elise squeezes her hand rather than answer aloud.

Together they lower their hands from aloft and bring the rain down with them.

At the last second, as the water reaches the ground, Nadia flicks her wrist sending a spray of water directly at Sala.

He is instantly drenched from head to toe.

Elise breaks down laughing as the rain just pours out of the cloud in front of them. This is maybe the sixth time Nadia has created a rainstorm today. Elise, however, is a quick study. Feeling her power makes Nadia want to learn hers better. The years of letting her power atrophy makes her angry. She should be proficient in these basics by now.

Elise squeezes her hand and doesn't let it go.

"Don't beat yourself up," she says softly. "It's not your fault."

She smiles wanly at her best friend. Together they walk over to where Sala is toweling off.

"I'd say that was a success," he says.

"So would I."

The latter comment comes from an approaching uniformed man with a colonel's bird on each shoulder. With him are two other uniformed officers, a woman with major six-pointed stars and a younger sergeant who is marked as a caster witch. The colonel gives Sala a loaded glance before turning to Nadia and Elise.

"Miss Oswald, we are pleased with your progress," the colonel says.

Sala makes the introductions. "This is Colonel Ergamenes. Colonel, may I present the writer witches Miss Nadia Oswald and Miss Elise Chulyin."

As per her training, Nadia salutes Colonel and he salutes back. He shakes Elise's hand saying, "You're from Umbra?"

"Yes, sir," Elise answers. "From Arcta."

"I went to Arcta on an exchange program for a year," he says. "It's a beautiful city."

"It is, thank you."

"Miss Oswald," the colonel says, "You will be commissioned as a corporal and will be required to work with the Weapons Spells Division."

Nadia is stunned. "You want me to create spells that will be weaponized, sir?"

"Given your lack of expertise, we feel you might be

able to write spells that are simple enough for any caster to use," he says. "This will be your task."

Nadia opens her mouth. She can feel Elise shift next to her. She is about to protest and without thinking better of it, she plunges forward. "Sir, I will not be participating in that manner. You may set me anywhere else within the armed services, but I will not create weaponized spells."

"I beg your pardon? This is not a request, Miss Oswald."

"And I am serious. I will be a conscientious objector if necessary, but I will not weaponize my spells," she says. "I will engineer, I will build, I will work the weather and all other manner of spellwork, but I will not weaponize my magic."

Colonel Ergamenes's jaw clenches, his face turning red.. Elise's hand gently brushes hers in a sign of solidarity. Nadia stands up straighter and remembers what Elise told her about being a natural anchor. She feels her stubbornness has something to do with it. And the way she is standing her ground now only confirms that feeling. She is a pacifist and she won't back down from this.

In that moment she feels something shift in the air

between her and the colonel. It is a feeling more than anything. It is just the sense of her standing still, rooted in place, and the colonel shuddering slightly as if he is pushed by an invisible breeze. And like a thin grass he has no choice but to bend to the wind.

"Alright Miss Oswald," he says. "We won't force you to join the Weapons Division just yet." The ominous tone suggests she has a fight ahead of her. "But be aware I am not the highest rung on the ladder and you will get those orders at some point. And if you do then choose to defy them, we can have you jailed for two years."

Nadia clenches her jaw. She knows she worked her anchor magic on him. But she doesn't know how well enough to feel confident she can do it again. "I understand, sir," she says.

"For now carry on with your training," he orders.

"Yes, sir."

And then he turns and leaves without another word to her. Sala seems to break out of his stunned silence and chases after him. Elise's hand goes between Nadia's shoulder blades. She feels her friend rub her back in a gesture of support and comfort.

"That was bravely done."

"Or stupidly."

"You used your power on him," she says. It's not a question.

"Yes," Nadia says. "But I'm going to have to get extremely good at it extremely quickly if I want to stay out of Weapons Division."

Elise hums in agreement. "You're going to have to get good at this if we have a hope of staving off this war."

And Nadia in that moment has an idea that she immediately forgets because Sala is coming back. There is no time to think about rogue ideas about how to prevent the coming war. They have more weatherwork to do.

Twenty-Nine

If he hadn't received the letter from Howells, Aidan would not have made the trip. If he hadn't been receiving steady notes from Nadia, he would not be motivated to go at all. As it stands both of those things are true. So he finds himself on the last leg of an excruciatingly long journey looking at the skyline of Port Nalrang.

Aidan steadies his horse as Porter rides up next to him. He had stopped so he could get a good look at the place from a distance again. The last time he was here he was an anchor witch. Now he would enter the place as a fire elemental.

"We can still turn back," Porter suggests.

His family had discouraged his trip when he stayed with them in Avita Spring. But he had explained that

Howells's messages seemed urgent and he had to meet with Nadia and Elise to see how they were getting along. Besides, the water table being so high in Avita Spring unsettles him now in a way he never expected it to. He imagines he will get used to it with time. For the moment he must just deal with the ever-present element that is so contrary to his own.

No he cannot turn back now. Howells needs him to come and introduce him to Nadia. And Nadia needs all the guidance she can get. He has responsibilities that scream in the face of his instinct to run away and live in the wild as a nomad. He still has things tethering him to the world of witches.

"We can't," he says simply. "I have responsibilities."

Porter nods either in agreement or out of respect.

Aidan urges his horse onward and they make their way across the last distance to the city itself. In the hour or so that passes he feels like he is entering a cage of steel and glass. He feels he is entering a place of closed in spaces where he could never let his element free.

Porter rings the bell at Nadia's building and waits for them to be let in. Their horses are taken from them and their luggage is hurried around to a back lift in the rear of the building. Porter walks ahead of Aidan as they are escorted through the magnificent vestibule into a space where the lifts come down to ground floor. They step onto the lift, the operator asking where they are going. The apartment has been rung ahead of them so that Nadia's family would not be surprised at their arrival.

They step off the lift on the ninth floor and step out into a hallway lined with lush carpet and lit with mini electric chandeliers along the hallway. Nadia's apartment is one of only four on this floor. It takes up a massive amount of the building's footprint. They find the door halfway down the hall. A wooden door that is ornate in its plainness. Wood itself is a luxury few can afford.

Porter rings the bell and they are greeted by a stout butler who ushers them in with little prelude. He takes their coats and leads them to the living room where he announces their arrival. There they find Nadia, Elise, and a man who could only be Nadia's father.

"Aidan!"

It is Elise who greets him so warmly first. She too had written, but the letters were more personal in nature.

They shake hands and then she pulls him into a hug.

"Have you recovered?" she asks.

"I am fully recovered now," he says. He smiles at her then turns to Nadia and greets her as well. "How are

you?"

"I am managing," she says. When their hands make contact, he feels a flair of recognition from her anchor power. The magic recognizes its former holder.

"Thank you for having us."

"Don't thank me," she says. "Thank my father." She gestures at the tall man waiting while the younger people greet each other. "Father, this is Aidan Montgomery. Aidan, this is my father, Edgar Oswald."

"Mr. Oswald," Aidan says, extending his hand. "I am sorry for your loss."

The words are kindly meant but he can see that there is unease at the mention of Nadia's dead mother. Rather than comment on it, her father simply says, "Thank you. And you are welcome here."

"I appreciate you hosting us."

Mr. Oswald smiles wryly. "It's not every day a rising politician hosts two witches and an elemental," he says. Nadia rolls her eyes but Mr. Oswald doesn't notice.

"I guess not."

"Salter will show you to the guest quarters," he says. "I'm sure you would like to settle in before attending to your responsibilities."

"Thank you."

The butler leads them down the hall with Nadia and Elise trailing them. They come to a side hallway—the place being even bigger than Aidan anticipated—and Salter leads them that way.

"We go this way," Nadia explains. "We'll see you for tea in a few minutes." She and Elise continue down the main hallway to the rooms in that direction.

Aidan gives an awkward half wave and heads down the hallway with Hughes. They find his luggage dusted off and set on a stand. Porter begins going through the luggage and getting his things set up in the wardrobe. Aidan goes to the washstand and splashes water on his face. The water doesn't feel good anymore, but at least it does the trick of getting some of the grit off. He dries his hands and face on a towel and turns back to Porter. The man ducks into the adjoining room to give Aidan space to change. Aidan takes advantage of the chance to get the dust off him.

Once he is in fresh trousers and a fresh shirt, Aidan turns back to the washstand mirror and tries his best to flatten his flyaway hair. It's no use though. He stares at the fluffy brown and sighs internally at his teenage appearance.

A candle on the washstand catches his attention for a

moment. He reaches out with one finger and does what he has now learned to do. He produces a single tiny flame. The candle lights. For a moment he just watches it, marveling at how easy that is compared to using witchcraft. It is a totally different beast to be a part of the element rather than simply calling it. He snuffs out the flame.

He finds the girls in a small parlor with two ornate couches and a few chairs, some heavy marble side tables and sconces on the walls. Several paintings of landscapes represent the plateau, the beaches to the south, and even one of Port Nalrang clearly painted from a boat in the Falgar.

"You like our art," Nadia says.

"I do. I think I like landscapes."

"They are all Josiah Gambrill, except of course the Port Nalrang seascape. That is by Rosie Lawry."

"You have an original Lawry?"

"Of course. My mother insisted one year."

The way she said it Aidan could hear the tension in her voice. He realizes that he doesn't know much about Nadia's relationship with her family. At least not more than that she hid her power for a long time. He takes a seat across from Nadia and Elise.

Nadia graciously serves everyone some tea and scones.

Elise smiles at Aidan. "How was the journey?"

Aidan smiles back and says, "Tiring. As you well know."

She nods and asks, "Did you stay with your family in Avita Spring?"

"Yes, I did," he says. "It was nice to see them again. It had been a couple months."

"And how are your powers coming along?"

"Slowly, which is good for an elemental," he says. "I don't want to lose control by being reckless."

"I can imagine."

"How are your powers coming along?"

Nadia interjects saying, "Elise is a prodigy."

"Is that so?"

Elise shrugs modestly. "I am picking it up, but I have the benefit of having a practiced power and immediate study."

Nadia gets up and sets the tea service on the side table and softly closes the door. The sounds from the rest of the house are completely cut off.

He raises his eyebrows. "Silencer?" he asks.

"An extremely simple one," she answers. "I'm not

very adept yet."

It's strange but the magic she used feels like a piece of music he has forgotten. He doesn't quite understand it anymore. He can just feel that she did something. He drinks a sip of the hot tea and sets those feelings aside. At least hot liquids feel soothing still. He takes a bite of the scone.

"Alright, let's really talk for a moment."

"At least while I can hold the spell in place," Nadia says.

"True," Elise replies. "How are you *really* doing, Aidan? I've been worried about you."

"You know about my original power?" he asks Elise. Nadia knows about his anchor power, but he isn't sure whether she told Elise.

"Nadia informed me," Elise says, confirming his suspicions. The Gag was never completely failproof. Even Goliyant isn't that good. It's no surprise to him that Nadia, with her own strong writer power, was able to beat the spell. She was the only one who ever saw through the spell in the first place.

Aidan sighs. He is tired and thus has no energy to put up a front for these two girls he is getting to know so well. "I want to run away," he says. "I want to leave everything behind and be free."

Elise nods. "I wrote to Hydris about this a little while ago," she said. "He manages to live among humans and witches pretty well. So I wanted to pass his insight on to you when I got the chance."

"I'm certainly interested," Aidan says. "I need to know how to work through this."

"That's the thing," Elise says. "It's not a matter of working through it. It's a matter of accepting the instincts the element gives you."

"You mean, don't fight them?"

"Not exactly," she says. "Make them a part of who you are."

Aidan pauses, then laughs softly. "It's funny because I feel more connected to my elemental power than I ever did to my anchor power," he says. "I feel chaotic by nature and fire is chaotic."

Nadia looks pensive. "That's how I feel. I feel settled, centered, and like I am in the right place," she says. "I feel more connection to your anchor power than I did with my writer power."

Aidan stares at her, feeling again that maybe she was right. That everything is as it should be.

"I need to introduce you to Howells while I'm here,"

he says. "He says it is urgent that we communicate."

"How about tomorrow afternoon?"

"That would be acceptable. We'll have to bring our escorts, but he won't like them to come up with us," Aidan says.

"Can I come?"

He smiles at Elise. "I don't see why not, he just doesn't like a lot of company."

A rap on the door catches all their attention. The door opens, breaking Nadia's spell. The butler Salter pokes his head through.

"Miss Nadia, your father needs you in his study. And I am to remind your guests we will have dinner in two hours," he says.

Nadia nods and thanks Salter. "Excuse me," she says to Aidan and Elise. "You're welcome to prepare for dinner. It will be informal tonight." She gets up and leaves the room. Aidan finds himself alone with Elise.

"How are you doing away from home," he asks Elise.

"It's warmer than I like," she says with a laugh. "I just don't think about it much to be honest. I'm too busy working with Nadia."

"Are you two partners?"

Elise looks thoughtful. "I'm not sure yet," she answers earnestly. "I think we work well together but I'm not sure we're there yet."

"My witch partner John is coming down to visit while I'm here in Port Nalrang," Aidan says. He had just missed John on his way through Courtthostur. He couldn't let the friendship or the partnership die just because he is no longer what he was.

"That's nice!" Elise says. "I don't know how to work together as a witch yet, but I've been helping Nadia for years."

"She said that at the meeting a few months back. I know how important you have been to her education," he says.

"I tried anyway. Which is more than most."

The door to the parlor opens again and Nadia steps through with a sigh.

"What is it?" Elise asks her.

"It was about the thing the other day," was the indecipherable response.

"Oh you mean how you could end up in jail."

Aidan looks at her in alarm.

"It's not that dramatic," Nadia says, sitting down next to Elise. "I just don't want to make weapons spells.

I want to help with the war effort, but I'll be a conscientious objector before they make me make a spell that kills."

"Bravo," Aidan says with gusto. "I'm not sure I would have the fortitude to do that."

Nadia blushes.

"I told you he'd be supportive."

"I think there might be another way," he says. "I mean if you want to use your power in other ways."

"Like as an anchor, how you and Howells did," she says.

"Perhaps."

"Well, we'll meet tomorrow," Nadia says. "In the meantime I'm going to change for dinner or face my father's disapproving looks."

A bell tolls in the apartment somewhere. Elise immediately gets up. "That's the dressing bell," she says. "We should be in the living room in an hour or so."

"I think I'll lay down for a few minutes," Aidan says. He really is tired. He knows tomorrow he'll feel stiff from riding the horse all day.

They walk down the hallway to where it divides and Aidan heads to his guest room. Once he shuts the door behind him, he lets out a deep sigh. He wonders how easy it will be to stop fighting with his power and learn to accept his abilities as part of his personality. It's just not that easy. He kicks off his boots and lays down on the bed. He thinks about all the changes he went through and the long day behind him. In that moment he knows he can't do this alone. So as much as he wants to wander off and leave everything behind, he can't and he won't.

Aidan drifts off to sleep.

Thirty

The following afternoon Nadia found herself venturing into a part of Port Nalrang her father would not normally approve of. He only made the exception this time because they were accompanied by three escorts. Escorts he did not know would be staying outside when they got to their destination. They are of course going to visit Howells, one of the main reasons Aidan came to Port Nalrang in the first place.

Aidan led them to West Prekrol, one of the oldest parts of Port Nalrang. Before there was a city, there were several small villages connected by dirt roads. The roads all connected to the harbor via a hairpin turning road carved from the cliffs down to the water. There, a tiny hamlet by the name of Nalrang grew into the bustling metropolis perched on the cliff tops. The hairpin road was cut even deeper into the cliff to allow for larger carts to make the trip. And just a decade ago a series of high-capacity lifts were completed to allow for easy transport from the coastal neighborhood up to the city proper.

West Prekrol occupies the furthest boundary of the city, a rundown part of town that used to be prosperous when they were simply a collection of villages. Now every building looks like it's about to fall down. Every resident they see hurries by and keeps their eyes away from others. Every home looks impoverished.

The old house turned apartment building Aidan leads them to has a door that is sitting off the hinges to one side. The three of them—Nadia, Aidan, and Elise—all get off their horses and leave the trio of escorts at the front of the building. None of them protest. The six of them had planned this out. And something about two witches and an elemental going in alone felt like they were adequately protected.

Inside Nadia is unsurprised to find the building in as much disrepair as it is. She can sense and occasionally see the magic holding the place together. It's subtle, woven into the fibers of the adobe bricks and into the metal making up the stairs. They make it upstairs to the third floor and find a door with the letter "H" on it. Aidan knocks.

A wild looking older man opens the door and hurries them inside. Nadia glances at Elise whose expression says more than anything.

"Aidan," the man who could only be Howells says. "I heard about your transition."

While Aidan introduces them and makes small talk, Nadia looks around the room, taking in the clutter of books and papers and the rickety cot in the corner and the chalkboard along the one wall. All of it screams disgraced academic and indeed that is what Howells is. A disgraced witch. An un-sought-after supposed writer witch whose concealment of his abilities was enough to disgrace him. Not even the military and the rest of the government want him now.

"So you're the new anchor witch," Howells says.

"Yes, I'm Nadia," she says.

"Yes, the Oswald girl." Howells gets uncomfortably close to Nadia peering into her eyes and inspecting her power with his own. She can feel the recognition of one anchor power to another and that alone is enough to tell her she is exactly what she is meant to be.

"You've settled."

Confused, Nadia looks to Aidan.

"He means you've settled into being an anchor. You are self-actualized enough to use the power efficiently."

"I wouldn't say 'efficiently'," Nadia says modestly. "But I'm using it."

"Anchor power is very black and white, Miss Oswald," Howells says. "You either use it or you don't, as Aidan can tell you."

"Call me Nadia please," she says. "And he has told me that."

"Alright, Nadia," Howells says, giving her more space. "And your friend has your old writer power?" he asks, now studying Elise.

"Yes," she says. "I got it when Nadia got the anchor power."

"*Because* Nadia got the anchor power," Howells says. "You three make a fantastic study for the Replacement Principle and the Rarity Conundrum. I would do a write up on you three if I could publish it. I should do it anyway and publish with the church."

"The witch's church?" Nadia asks.

Elise glances at Nadia. Nadia had explained about it—what little she knows—when they had first had the powers move.

"Yes," Howells says. "They know I am an anchor,

but they don't like that I won't reveal all the identities of anchors to them."

Aidan snorts in an uncouth manner. "I'm sorry, but that's not their choice."

"Precisely."

"I would ask if you would both consent to having your statuses added to the registry," he says looking back and forth between Aidan and Nadia. The two of them look at each other and shrug.

Nadia turns to Elise who says, "I don't mind being known as a writer witch, but it's your decision how much you're willing to tell."

"I need to think about it," Nadia says. "I promise I will have an answer for you."

"Would it still be alright if I interviewed you three about the power shift?"

"At some point, for sure."

"Either way," Aidan says, "we're here so Nadia can learn how to anchor populations."

The sudden change of topic doesn't faze Howells who merely begins shuffling through a stack of papers. From his behavior and the scattered nature of the room, Nadia guesses that he possesses mental divergence of some kind. Howells comes up with a piece of thick parchment with what she can see are a series of equations written on them. He hands her the paper.

Nadia is good at math, but this is beyond her.

"Let me take a look," Elise says. Nadia hands her the parchment. After a few minutes of reading through it, Elise asks, "This symbol here means . . . ?"

"That is the witch's constant. The mathematical symbol for it anyway."

"What about this?"

"That is the symbol I use to indicate the human soul."

"Ah, the circle being the human and the line being the soul?" she asks.

"Yes."

"Okay I think I understand." To Nadia Elise says, "He's suggesting using your witch's constant and the basic human soul connection to calm a mass of people. Am I correct?" she adds to Howells.

"You are adept at mathematics."

"I try. I went to the witch's conference a couple months ago."

"You met Wilhelm then."

"Yes."

"And you took the math seminars." It wasn't a

question. To the trained eye, it was obvious that Elise had mathematics knowledge beyond her level of school.

"I enjoyed them."

"You must be a good writer witch then." With a pause and a look of consideration, Howells says, "You can help."

"Thanks," Elise says, looking strangely at Howells. To Nadia it felt that Elise did not expect that. But Elise is the genius between the two of them. She should be helping.

"When do we start?"

"This is best done at midnight. We will start with the population of Port Nalrang to get you warmed up. Then we can talk about doing a bigger populous."

The idea of working on all of Port Nalrang feels daunting. Nadia suddenly feels unstable within. Then her anchor power rises up within her and she finds her steadiness again. And her power sits there simmering within her, ready to be used.

"How big? Enough to stop the war?"

"I don't know," Howells admits. "With just the two of us, I don't know."

A silence lapses between them. Aidan is getting antsy being stuck inside.

"When should we return?" Nadia asks.

"I will make preparations. Return in two days, just before midnight," Howells says.

Nadia and Elise look at each other, nodding subtly about how no matter what they would make the trip possible. And Aidan nods as well, his hands twitching at being inside.

"Shall we head back?"

"Yes," Aidan says. "I have some energy to burn off, so I may go to the proving grounds."

"Don't let your element control you, Aidan," Howells says. "It's the same with witchcraft after all."

Aidan nods, but the look of concern on his face makes Nadia wonder how much he needs that kind of reminder. "I am trying to understand who I am now," he says. "And incorporate it into myself." The look he gives Elise with those words makes Nadia wonder. She knows Elise had been doing research on elementals for him, so she wonders if they had had a conversation.

"We should go," Elise says. "Howells, it was a pleasure to meet you."

"You as well, Miss Chulyin."

Elise extends a hand to him and says, "Please call me Elise. I look forward to continuing our correspondence."

Then she blinks in surprise at the statement. "I mean . . ."

Howells gives her an appraising smile. "So you are able to use your seer abilities after all."

"I guess so."

"Howells, see you in a couple days." Nadia shakes his hand as well, feeling the flare of recognition from her power.

They make their way out of the small apartment with Aidan bringing up the rear. They are silent as they move through the old building. Aidan carefully swings the door shut behind them, it barely hanging on the hinges. It then occurs to Nadia that maybe he shouldn't be touching something so flammable.

"How did it go?" Kaye asks her as she mounts her horse.

"We need to come back in two days, at midnight," she says simply.

Kaye's eyebrows go up but he doesn't ask anything further.

They make their way back to the other side of town.

Thirty-One

A knock on the door wakes Aidan in the early hours the next day.

"Wake up," Porter says, coming into his room. "There's a representative from the military here for both you and Miss Oswald."

All grogginess at being woken too early leave Aidan in a jolt. Suddenly he is so wide awake he can't even think about sleep.

"For both of us?"

"Yes."

"Why?"

"I don't know," Porter says. "There was a witchwire this morning that unsettled Mr. Oswald. I did not see it."

Aidan gets out of bed and throws on the clothes Porter hands him. Every piece of clothing has been replaced with flame-retardant clothing. While the fire wouldn't burn Aidan anyway, the clothes wouldn't turn to ash as quickly at least. At least he had the peace of mind that he wasn't going to end up stark naked if his flames got a little overzealous. Fully dressed in his new clothes he headed out of the bedroom to the living area.

Nadia is already there when he arrives. Elise sits on a chaise to the side but Nadia is pacing, unable to stay still. Two men also wait for them, both dressed in full military gear, one a Colonel and the other a Lieutenant. Nadia's father stands to one side, nodding at Aidan as he comes in.

"Mr. Montgomery?" the Colonel says.

"Yes, Colonel."

"We require your services. There is a contingent of troops from Ecrium crossing the Falgar and on their way here within the next two days."

"You want me to use my fire on the water, sir?"

"If possible," he says. "I understand that new elementals can cope with their opposite element. We are hoping you will be able to use your power from a ship."

Aidan blinks. The idea of standing on a boat in the middle of the Falgar makes him nauseous. There isn't much he can do to argue. As an elemental of Egraria, he is obligated to participate in state activities.

"I will certainly try, sir."

"Good," the Colonel says. "We will get you out to the ship early so you can practice if necessary." He says it as if he thinks Aidan will not need the practice.

Then the Colonel turns to Nadia and says, "Are we going to have a problem?"

Nadia openly glares at the Colonel. "I stand by what I said. I will not write spells that will be used to kill."

Aidan can feel the rumbling of Nadia's anchor power just below the surface. His own fire waits, sits quiet, waiting for him to call it. Aidan clenches a fist to remind himself what could happen if he loses control.

"Miss Oswald, you are obligated to serve."

"And I will serve in any other way than that."

The force in her voice stuns the room.

"Nadia," her father hisses. "This is Colonel Ergamenes you are talking to. Show some respect."

"Only if you will respect my decision." There is pause. "Sir," she adds belatedly.

"This is not a question of your decision," the Colonel says. "You are a conscript and you *will* obey orders."

Tense silence fills the room. The Colonel exchanges

a look with the Lieutenant and nods. The Lieutenant steps forward.

"Miss Oswald," he says, "By order of the Sanction Arm of his majesty's army, you will comply with the orders given or you will be thrown into military prison for a sentence of no less than two years."

"Now just one minute," Mr. Oswald says. "Nadia is still a minor."

"Yes," the Colonel says, "but she is a conscript. Since she is a minor, you are also responsible for her actions and can be fined and imprisoned as well."

Nadia looks at her father with a stubborn expression. "I will not do it."

"Is there some agreement we can come to? Some alternate work she can do?"

"This is not a negotiation," the Colonel says. "She will do what she is told or you both will be imprisoned."

"I will not, sir," she says. "I will be a conscientious objector. I will not condone the use of my power for violence."

Part of him knows it's the power within her talking. An anchor values all the lives around them. Values them enough to want to protect them. Even those viewed as an enemy have value to an anchor. She would be fighting her instincts and her power to produce spells that could kill. He sympathizes with her but can't see a way for her to get out of it.

"We don't have space for conscientious objectors in our ranks."

"You will now, sir," she retorts.

The Colonel bristles.

"Enough Nadia!" her father snaps. "You will not do this. You will comply with the Colonel's orders."

"I will not kill or produce spells that can be used to kill." The strength of her power comes through in her voice. The power commands the room, making even Aidan stand up straighter and recognize it. "I will help in other ways, but I will not be used as an instrument of death."

For a moment he looks like he might back down, but instead he sticks to his convictions.

"You will follow orders or you will be imprisoned. Weapons are the only way to defeat the Ecrium forces coming. You cannot defeat them with weather spells and calm persuasion."

Aidan glances over at Nadia. She has stopped pacing. Her eyes aren't focused on anything but he sees a look of determination come over her face. And then her face goes calm. Aidan's stomach turns over as she makes eye contact with him. Something shifted in her and she is not the complaining rebelling girl she was a moment ago.

"I think we're done here," the Colonel says. "Report to the proving grounds tomorrow morning. We don't have any time to waste."

"Thank you, Colonel," Nadia's father says.

The conversation ends there with the Colonel and the Lieutenant leaving. Nadia leaves the room as well, not bothering to even acknowledge her father. Elise follows and Aidan excuses himself.

He feels badly for Nadia. It seems she is always subject to another's whims. Her mother before her father. The military now. He wonders if she reached her breaking point.

Then he wonders if he will reach his.

Thirty-Two

Nadia made the decision understanding she is taking an incredible risk to do so. She isn't going to help them kill people. She isn't going to change who she is for the sake of the military.

She shakes Elise awake in the middle of the night. She holds one finger over her lips to keep her friend quiet. It's not midnight yet. The whole house is quiet.

"What is it?" Elise whispers.

"I know what to do. Get dressed. We're going to the beach."

Elise's eyes go wide in the dim light. She doesn't question her best friend. She just gets up and begins putting on clothes.

Nadia knows she needs Aidan's help but she can't just go knock on his door at this hour. So she does the

only thing she can think of. She uses his old anchor witch power to reach him. She is not adept at witchspeak enough to initiate it. Nor would she know how to target him with it. The best she can do is reach out with her power and hope he wakes to meet her.

"Nadia?" Aidan says in witchspeak, forming the connection with her.

"Aidan, we need to go."

There is a pause. Then he says, *"I'll meet you at the front door."*

For some reason they trust each other. Maybe because they have held the same power and feel the echoes of the power between them. She knows he wonders what she is doing, but he must also trust her decisions.

Finally she rings the bell for Kaye. As they dress, he comes and pokes his head in her room. She whispers, "Meet us at the front door." He doesn't ask questions and merely nods and leaves the room.

At the front door she sees that the three of them have chosen to dress in their witch training clothes. The practicality of it is what struck her. Even Kaye, standing at the door waiting on them, is dressed in a similar, practical way.

Quietly, the group opens and closes the front door and makes their way to the lift. They stand in complete silence as the four of them head down to the ground floor. The guard on duty has dozed off and doesn't even see them leaving the building. They walk down the street to the stalls and steam carriages. Kaye signals for them all to get into the Oswald's steam carriage and they pile in the tiny vehicle. He starts the engine and hops into the driver seat, the sputtering of the engine extra loud in the quiet night air.

Kaye drives them through the streets of the downtown area and heads to the east. The city is quiet for it being late in the night on Epday. Usually the end of the week is bustling, but Nadia supposes the attacks and the protests and even the impending forces from Ecrium are keeping everyone at home. Even the shops and restaurants that would normally be open are all closed and shuttered tight. They are the only carriage on the roads and the feeling is creepy to Nadia.

They pass out of the downtown area and head through the Drissald Yard and through Sossagand East, the old village set on the precipice of the cliff road. Kaye takes the first turn down the cliff road, turning on the carriage's front lights in the process. Nadia's father paid for the best carriage he could get and most don't have front lights. Driving down the cliff road, Nadia is grateful for her father's pride and excess.

By the time they reach the coastal neighborhood, Epeths is high in the night sky, a glittering full moon giving them some light on their path. They drive through the quiet town, a town that had been partially evacuated due to the coming forces from Ecrium. As they approach the water, Nadia can see the growing forces accumulating around the docks. How they would get a boat out in the midst of all this Nadia doesn't know. But Kaye apparently has a plan.

He parks the carriage in a side alley and signals for everyone to be silent. They follow him without a word, only the sound of their boots on the pavement to mark their passage. He goes around the corner to another part of the port. Here there are dozens of small ships, all privately owned by those who live in the more affluent part of Nalrang. Her father's modest sailboat is one of them.

They hide in the shadow of all the ships, dodging from boat to boat. Then they are at her father's boat. And they climb aboard while Kaye casts them off. He hops in at the last minute and he takes the helm. Nadia and Elise and Aidan all row together to get the boat away from the dock and out into the bay proper. Then they are far enough that Kaye starts the tiny engine. They hear shouts from the shore but it's too late. The coastline recedes behind them.

At one point Nadia looks over at Aidan and sees he is barely coping with the water under them. He is sitting in the middle of the boat, as far from the edges as possible.

"Are you alright?" she asks.

"I'll be fine, but it takes some getting used to."

Nadia nods. Kaye keeps them going out into the water. Elise watches behind them.

"We better do this soon. They won't take long to catch up to us."

Nadia follows Elise's gaze. What looks like three boats are following them, their front lights casting beams across the water. Kaye makes the turn out of the bay. The cliffs still hunch over them, tall and overbearing. He pulls the boat into the shadow of the cliff nearest and cuts the engines. The pursuing boats go right past out into the open waters of the Falgar.

"I think this is as far as we get," Kaye says.

"It's far enough," Nadia says, looking around. Part

of her is afraid of going too far to sea. She pulls a piece of paper out of her pocket, the scratchy sketch the best she could replicate from the design Howells showed them. She hands it to Aidan.

"This is good," he says, his eyebrows going up. "I think you've got most of it."

"Do you think it'll be enough? Even if I missed something?"

"With the three of us here? I hope it's enough."

Elise takes the sketch. She takes a piece of chalk from Nadia and begins sketching the diagram on the boat deck. As she's drawing the circles, she makes a few adjustments.

"How did you know to do that?"

Elise shrugs. "Math, of course. It's just a series of circles all secant to each other except for the one you stand in. That one should be tangent."

Nadia squints at the diagram as it's coming together. "That's what Howells was doing," she mutters. Geometry was never Nadia's strongest subject, but she understands it enough that calculus was never an issue. If she wanted to, she could probably calculate the equations of the circles. But they didn't have time for that and she didn't want to.

"All done."

Elise stands up and dusts off her hands. She added two tangential circles for her and Aidan to stand in. Aidan's face looks uncomfortable as he takes his place near the side of the boat.

"Ready?"

"As ready as I'll ever be."

"Just don't fight it," Aidan says. "Don't fight who you are and it'll do the work for you."

Nadia nods, tightens her ponytail, and swallows just once. She steps into her circle. She lifts her hands to the diagram. Nadia begins the spell.

The power she draws is greater than anything she has attempted, but the scope of this spell goes beyond anything she could have imagined. So she pulls her power from deep within, pulling every ounce of magic she can. The diagram glows softly in the moonlight, the chalk picking up some of her power. Through the connection to the main circle, she can feel the power within Elise and Aidan. The controlled precision of Elise's writer power and the wild unruliness of Aidan's elemental power feed into the spell, woven together with Nadia's grounded anchor power.

Her hands begin to glow with power. Her body feels

the energy draining out of her, but she keeps pushing, keeps going knowing it would take everything she has. Elise and Aidan are doing the same, pushing as much power as they can into the spell. She knows all three of them will probably need to sleep for two days after this.

Together the three of them move in tandem, each raising their hands upward towards the moon in the night sky. Nadia holds their collective power there for as long as she can. She lets the power build up until it is so strong she can barely keep it in check. She lifts her gaze to the heavens. Then she says the words, her voice echoing in witchspeak.

"Peace to all. Return home now."

She lets the power go. The diagram flashes.

Nadia collapses onto the boat deck. Both Elise and Aidan bend over in exhaustion.

"Nadia, are you ok?"

"I'm still here," she says to Elise.

"Did it work?"

"I guess we'll find out." She peels herself off the deck and looks up at Kaye whose face is filled with concern. "We should get home."

Kaye starts the engine.

A spotlight hits the boat.

Aidan swears and so does Elise. The words seem incomprehensible coming from her.

"Shut your engine," a voice calls out over a speech magnifier.

"We're in trouble."

The three of them cluster on the boat. All they can do is wait for the boats to reach them and the consequences to come weighing down. Nadia takes both their hands, feeling she needs the support.

"We'll get through this."

"I hope so."

Thirty-Three

"What do you *mean* you're an anchor witch?"

Aidan does not know how Nadia is holding her own against the cluster of military officers, some of whom she clearly knows. He and Elise sit to her left at a conference table in a claustrophobic room with gray walls. None of them has slept. They were taken straight to Conscription Authority headquarters and brought to this room. Nadia's father had been notified and currently sits next to her as their lawyer. It is possible he and Nadia could face military charges.

Nadia sighs, barely able to stay awake after all the power she put out. She goes to speak again, but Aidan decides he needs to step in.

"It's like this," he begins. "We don't reveal ourselves because it is dangerous. As far as I know there are only about a half a dozen in the world, and I have no idea who most of them are."

"Because it's dangerous," Colonel Ergamenes repeats what Nadia said earlier.

"Yes. Writers are already targets. Think how much more of targets anchors would be if they were known generally."

"The Rarity Conundrum." The words come from Arnaldo Sala. Half the people in the room are witches, but he seems the most sympathetic.

"Yes," Aidan says. "We're taking a risk even revealing this to you."

"Because you were the anchor before Nadia."

"She got my power when I became an elemental, yes," he continues. "And Elise has Nadia's old writer power. It's just always been safer to pose as a writer or caster witch. Most people, certainly almost all humans, do not know that anchor witches exist. And it should be kept that way."

The Colonel exchanges looks with his peers. They step back from the table to talk quietly amongst themselves. Sala looks over Nadia appraisingly, probably thinking of all the power she has and how much sense it makes now.

Aidan exchanges glances with Nadia and Elise. At least Elise is fairly safe in all this, being Umbrian and a new writer witch. That is a small consolation, but a consolation nonetheless.

"Alright, here is how this is going to go," Colonel Ergamenes says. "We will all sign silence agreements and this will remain a confidential affair. Only those of us in this room will be aware of what you all are or were." He signals to his assistant. The sergeant hovering along the wall nods and steps out of the room. "*If* and only if your spell worked, you will be required to work in the Weapons Division to make this spell more targeted."

"No," Nadia growls. "Don't you get it? This only works *because* it's not a weapon. It's the *opposite* of a weapon."

"You will still work with them."

"No. And it wouldn't matter anyway. Only an anchor can use the spell."

Ergamenes looks back and forth between the three of them.

"She's right," Aidan says. "It's not a spell in the same sense that weathercasting is. It's an inherent ability of the anchor."

Colonel Ergamenes looks absolutely miffed. His

face is turning red and he is barely controlling himself. He looks like he wants to leap across the table at them. Especially at Nadia.

Aidan looks at her. The smug smile on her face is absolutely infuriating to Ergamenes. Aidan feels nothing but admiration for the way she's standing her ground. She doesn't want to be a weapon. And she's not going to stop until she gets her way. Ergamenes is not backing down either. They are at a stalemate.

"Then what exactly is your proposed solution to this, Miss Oswald?" Ergamenes seethes. The fact that he is even asking their opinion says they've won somehow.

"Exactly what I've been suggesting," she says. "Non-lethal spells and work that requires the use of an anchor's abilities."

Aidan works to keep from smiling at the way Ergamenes steps back from the table like he's been slapped. He exchanges a look with Elise. She can't keep the look of pride and amusement off her face. Looking at her almost made Aidan lose his self-control and burst out laughing.

Nadia's father steps forward and puts a hand on her shoulder. Aidan looks up at him and the man glances down for a second. There is a mixture of anger and pride in his eyes, a look he wasn't expecting to see. Nadia's father could be so adversarial to her that the fire in Aidan flares whenever he is around them both. At the moment the fire within feels warm and strong but not out of control. For a moment he wonders if he's learning to master it. Then his attention goes back to the matter at hand.

"My daughter is not your puppet. Yes, she is military. Yes, she is a witch fulfilling her duty," Mr. Oswald says. "But that does not give you the right to bully her or treat her like a tool or some piece of garbage. She is a powerful witch and you will respect her wishes."

"You have no right to say that," Ergamenes says directly to Mr. Oswald.

"The law is on her side, gentlemen," Mr. Oswald says smugly. "My daughter does not need my help to fight her battles." Aidan notices Nadia sits up a little straighter at those words. "But the law is on her side and I am her lawyer. I will fight for her right to act in non-lethal ways."

Rather than rebut Mr. Oswald, Colonel Ergamenes looks at his peers, the other Colonel and the miscellaneous majors and lieutenants none of whose names Aidan remembers. The other Colonel, a stout man with gray hair and wrinkles around his eyes, waves Ergamenes back into the group once again.

Aidan's shoulders relax a bit and he leans back into his chair. Mr. Oswald releases his daughter's shoulder and takes a seat next to her.

"Is that true?" Nadia whispers to him.

"It's all true," Mr. Oswald says. "You are well within your rights to defy them. It took some digging but there are several other cases that set the precedent for a conscientious objector. Even a very powerful one." His expression never changes. He remains the aloof lawyer so practiced at logical argument. Even though this is the most personal case he would ever have to fight.

One glance at Elise and he sees her eyebrows are up in surprise. He looks a questions at her. She shakes her head slightly. Later, they would talk about it later.

Another major enters the room holding a sheaf of papers which he hands to the stout Colonel. The man's bushy eyebrows go up and he shoves the pages into Ergamenes's hand. The Colonel leaves Ergamenes with his mouth agape in astonishment. He approaches the table.

"Miss Oswald, how much of your power would you say you used last night?"

The question surprises them all. It takes Nadia a moment to find the words to respond, but Aidan could have answered for her.

"Everything I could," she answers. "Why?"

"What about you Mr. Montgomery and Miss Chulyin?"

Aidan shakes his head. "Same. As much as I could stand."

"Me too," Elise says. "I don't know how to hold back yet."

The Colonel straightens up and looks at them appraisingly. He seems to hesitate for a moment but then plunges forward and explains.

"I have colleagues, my counterparts in other countries that I have regular contact with," he says. "We communicate nearly daily and this morning I received a witchwire from several of them. They all reported detecting an energy surge around the time of your spell last night." He pauses and puts out a hand for the sheaf of papers. He glances down at them and says, "The farthest report comes from Aprana, but I haven't heard from the north yet."

Aidan's jaw drops. "Aprana?" The country sits next to a lake in the southern hemisphere, some two thousand kilometers from Egraria.

"Yes. Aprana, Rebluinia, Namore. I even have a report from inside Ecrium that the energy surge was heavily detected there."

A thought occurs to Aidan. "Do you have a map?" he asks.

"What kind?"

"Global if possible."

One of the lieutenants pops out and comes back in with a rolled-up piece of paper. He spreads it open on the table and uses their water glasses as paperweights for the corners. Aidan stands up and hunches over the table. He finds the point he's looking for, hoping he's not wrong about this thought.

"We were here," he says, pointing to the Nalrang peninsula, the bay sitting behind it. The lieutenant hands him a pencil. Aidan marks a small "X" on the spot. "The spell is not haphazard," he explains. "It goes in the direction you send it. Where were the ships last night, the forces from Ecrium?"

The lieutenant takes the pencil back and makes several dots saying, "Here, here, and here." The marks are all due south of the X.

"Let's say our aim was good," Aidan says. He takes

the pencil back. He draws two lines forming a cone or a beam coming from the X and in the direction of the points. He carries the lines across the Falgar and into the southern hemisphere. Just as he thought, the lines encompass all the countries the Colonel listed.

"I don't think you're going to get reports from the north," Aidan says. "I think our aim was true and the reports you are getting are the remnants of our spell." He hands the pencil back to the lieutenant before he accidentally sets the wood on fire. Likewise he takes his hands off the parchment. His excitement at figuring this out is making him doubt his control again.

Colonel Ergamenes has joined them at the table along with two of the majors. The man has an inscrutable look on his face. He says, "Whether you like it or not, the spell is a weapon. It certainly directs like one."

Nadia comprehensively rolls her eyes next to Aidan. "You don't give up, do you?" she asks.

"Neither do you, apparently."

"Gentlemen, it's been a long night," Mr. Oswald says. "Can you release them so they can get some sleep?" By this point, it is after four in the morning.

The stout Colonel nods and says, "I think that

should be fine. Get some rest. I want to see you all at ten hundred hours. I expect you to give me details of your spell."

Aidan's eyes go between the Colonel and Ergamenes. "You mean he won't be working with us?"

The Colonel's eyes wrinkle further as he smiles. "You've demonstrated an adversarial relationship with him. I doubt a continued working relationship would be productive."

Ergamenes rolls his eyes.

Nadia stands up and extends her hand to the Colonel. "Nadia Oswald."

"Colonel Lawrence Cunningham." He shakes her hand.

Aidan and Elise follow Nadia's lead and stand up to shake his hand as well.

"Miss Chulyin, you should know the Umbrian government requests you contact them at your earliest convenience."

"Are they going to make me go home?" she asks.

"I don't believe so," the Colonel says. "It was something about having you officially registered. You left before you could do so, I believe."

Elise nods knowingly. "Yes, we did."

"Well, you can't be on a military exchange if you're not a registered member of the Umbrian army."

"Oh," Elise says in surprise. "I suppose that is what I'm doing here."

"Yes," Colonel Cunningham says. "Just make sure we can get it all done above board." He heads for the door but turns back for a moment to add, "Oh and Miss Oswald, if you complete your training, you will be commissioned as a second lieutenant." In the stunned silence, he leaves the room with Ergamenes trailing after him.

"Let's go before they change their minds, huh?" Mr. Oswald says.

In full agreement, they get up from the table and head out the door themselves. They pile into Mr. Oswald's steam carriage where Kaye is waiting. The man tips his hat at the three of them and then drives them back home.

Thirty-Four

Nadia pulls the covers back over her head and groans at the sunlight coming into her room. A responding groan comes from Elise's bed across the room and she sighs emphatically at being awake. The light in the window is barely past dawn. She did not bother closing the curtains last night as she knew they would need to be up early to deal with Colonel Cunningham.

Finally after much delay and internal resistance, she throws the covers off of her and swings her feet over the side of the bed. She gets up, slipping into her fluffy slippers, and makes her way to her private water closet, a perk of being an only child. Behind her Elise stirs as well, pulling on her morning robe.

After her morning routine, she leaves the water closet for Elise to use and pulls out her usual training gear to get dressed in. She is so exhausted after last night that every muscle feels heavy and every limb is a deadweight. Even the act of getting dressed is difficult as her concentration keeps slipping. Elise comes out of the water closet and similarly dresses in her witch gear. If all goes well at the Umbrian consulate later, she should have a commission in the Umbrian regime by dinnertime. Then she'll have the practical uniform of an Umbrian to wear while she goes about her witch business.

They head down the hall to the dining room for a light breakfast. Her father is far too awake-looking, having gotten some sleep before the Conscription Authority woke him around one in the morning. Aidan looks half-dead across the table. He cautiously lifts a cup of tea to his lips, looking dubiously at the vessel as if he might at any moment set the thing on fire. Nadia cannot imagine the strain of controlling a wild element like fire. She is glad she doesn't have to.

"Eat your breakfast, Nadia," her father says without even looking up from his paper. He doesn't have to look up to know she isn't eating. Annoyingly her father does know her pretty well. She drinks her tea and butters a slice of toast. She is not hungry yet, but she will likely burn some energy today. She needs to eat something to help her hold out till lunchtime.

The clock on the wall chimes the hour. It is now just nine o'clock in the morning. Nadia controls the sigh she wants to let out. She only got a few hours of sleep.

Her glance falls on Elise and the teacup the girl is drinking from. For a moment she flashes back to Coreton and their many trips to tea shops all over the town. She loses herself in the memory of those times and the freedom and security she felt despite not having any control over her then-writer witch power. The freedom she felt spending so much time with Elise and the two of them living their lives unencumbered by responsibility.

"Nadia," her father says in a warning voice, "Stop staring at your girlfriend's breakfast and eat your own."

The blush that spreads across Nadia's cheeks makes its way down her neck and collarbone and to her ears. Across the table Aidan merely lifts an eyebrow, his eyes going between the two of them. Neither Nadia nor Elise says a word. Nadia suddenly takes a deep interest in her eggs and toast, choosing to stare at them instead.

Some minutes pass. Nadia's father folds his newspaper. He glances at the clock, now reading ten after the hour. He glances around at all of them. Nadia takes a last deep drink of tea, seeing the rest have finished their breakfasts.

"We should get going," Nadia's father says.

"You're coming with us?" Nadia says, nearly choking on her tea.

"Until your legal troubles are resolved, I will be accompanying you to training, yes." He does not sound thrilled about the idea. He is, after all, going to give up his busy schedule of political and legal work to be their guardians.

"I thought it was resolved," Aidan says.

"You have no legally binding document or court ruling to protect you," her father says. "I am having my office write up a legal absolution for the Conscription Authority to sign off on. It will absolve you of your illegal activities last night." He stands up. "Enough of that for now. We need to go."

The three of them get up from the table and make their way to the foyer. There Kaye and Porter are waiting for them. Salter has coats ready for them. The morning air in Port Nalrang can be crisp. Then they head out the door and down to the lower garage where Kaye starts her father's horseless carriage. Like last night they simply pile into the carriage and Kaye begins driving.

The drive takes longer in Nadia's mind. Perhaps it is

because she is so tired and still drained from last night. It is a wonder she is awake at all. Her mind wanders at the simplest stray thought. Then they arrive and her focus comes back as they make their way through the Conscription Authority. This time they are led to a waiting room outside another, less imposing conference room. The four of them sit in plush chairs in silence.

She glances over at Aidan who is visibly uncomfortable, whether with the enclosed space or the ample amount of flammable items Nadia can't be sure. He shifts in his seat, glancing at her and offering a wan smile.

"Miss Oswald?"

They all look up. One by one they follow the speaker into the conference room. There, a half dozen military wait for them, one in a distinctly different uniform in a dusty blue coloring. Nadia nods cordially to Colonel Cunningham and Sala. She approaches and stands behind the center chair on the opposite side of the table from them.

"Please take a seat," Colonel Cunningham invites them. Once seated, he continues. "Please be aware this is unusual and we have a lot of business to get through before you continue training."

"Understood."

"First off, this is Major Ifren Radi of the Umbrian Military. He is a guest here at the behest of the Umbrian Consulate. If you are prepared, he will conscript you, Miss Chulyin."

Elise nods and affirms that she is ready.

"Then we'll do that last. For now we must discuss the delicacy of your secret Miss Oswald. And the safety of you and all other anchors," Colonel Cunningham says. "I gather from our conversation last night you will not be revealing the identities of any other anchors?"

"You are correct," Nadia answers. "For their sake as well as mine, I think it is best if you don't know and don't attempt to find out. I *know* you will try. But I assure you from this day forward I will have no contact with any other anchor. You all have robbed me of that."

"You are choosing that, Miss Oswald."

"No," she says. "If you were trustworthy with their names, you would not be pushing me. I know better than anyone the price of rare power. I know the danger posed by everyone, including you."

"Are you implying we would try to steal their power? Or yours?"

Nadia tilts her head to the side and says, "Perhaps

not you specifically. But yes, I do believe that."

Colonel Cunningham studies her for a moment, meeting her steely gaze with his own. He seems to be considering her words. Finally he shifts in his chair and looks uncomfortable as he says, "Fine. No one will push you or seek out the identities of the anchors you know. I can easily elucidate the danger of your power. So we have already classified the information you gave us last night. No one beyond that room and this is cleared for that knowledge. Satisfied?"

"Partially. I'd like to know my friends will be protected as well."

"We were about to get to that." He shuffles some papers in front of him and says, "We will be commissioning you and Mister Montgomery as officers and I believe Major Radi will be doing the same for you, Miss Chulyin."

Major Radi nods his head and answers in an Umbrian accent much thicker than Elise's. "If you accept commission in the military, you will be an officer as well."

Elise nods next to Nadia, a serious expression on her face. She asks, "Will I have to leave Egraria?"

Major Radi shakes his head. "I understand your partner is here," he says, his eyes going to Nadia and back to Elise. "While we will call you home for work periodically, there are enough writer witches available to borrow for now. You can be deployed in Egraria for familial reasons."

Nadia and Elise exchange a look and don't say anything. Everyone always assumes they are a couple, and there is truth to it, but they themselves had never discussed the parameters of their relationship. However, and this is where Nadia knows they agree, to call themselves family is not only accurate but welcome.

"That would be preferred," Elise says. She doesn't elaborate.

"Since that is settled, let's get started with the formalities."

Nadia's father takes the reins and begins to steer the meeting. The first real order of business is to assure the agreement exonerates them. Her father is the only one truly capable of doing that. But Nadia is not interested in legalese and tunes them out almost immediately. Elise reaches over and squeezes her hand as if in solidarity. At least half an hour passes with them all listening to the back and forth between Nadia's father and the various military on the other side of the table. After they are done, Colonel Cunningham calls for a much-needed recess. He tells them where to go freshen up and take a break if needed and says they will be sworn in after the recess. Nadia steps out of the room with Elise, Aidan following suit but heading to the restroom.

Elise's voice is soft when she finally asks the question. "Are we girlfriends?"

Nadia studies her, looking for any sort of reluctance or guile. But it is Elise. Their relationship is one of open trust. Communication is something they are good at. "I think so," Nadia answers.

"I think so too."

"Why have we never talked about this?" Nadia asks.

Elise shrugs. "I don't think we ever needed to before."

"And now our futures depend somewhat on being a couple." A couple of what, though. Friends? That really wasn't right. Girlfriends didn't even capture everything they had been through either. But it was the only word that seemed suited to their match.

Elise takes her hand again, this time holding it softly and studying Nadia's expression as she does so. "I like you. I always have. I don't know how much, but I'm willing to find out."

The words are enough for Nadia. And there in the

hallway of the Conscription Authority, with people passing them as they go about their business, Nadia reaches a hand up to Elise's cheek and kisses her. It was just once and it was over so quickly. But the flash of fire and light she got from it told her all she needed to know.

Then the recess is over and they are being called back in to go through swearing in. But from that day forward, everything would change.

Thirty-Five

Aidan woke the next morning with a slight headache but a sense of optimism he hadn't felt since he became an elemental. For some reason he didn't feel as if he would, at any moment, set the place on fire. He felt depleted still, but not as exhausted as he was the day before. The sleep had done him some good.

The room still dark, he reaches for the bedside candle and lights it with a fingertip. The marvel of fire just coming at his command has not worn off and probably wouldn't for a while. The room illuminates with the warm glow of candlelight, he peels himself out of bed and goes through his morning routine. With fresh fire-proof military clothes on and feeling a bit more awake, he extinguishes the light and heads for the common rooms.

Nadia and Elise look up as he enters the dining

room, seemingly startled out of deep conversation. For a moment he considers backing out the way he came and giving them space, but then Nadia greets him and he joins them.

"How are you this morning?"

Aidan shrugs. "Still adjusting."

"I know the feeling."

Elise nods in agreement.

"What were you two talking about, if I may ask?"

The two exchange a look and Nadia only says, "Parameters."

Before Aidan can ask any questions, they are interrupted by Nadia's father coming in. He takes his usual seat at the head of the table and looks around at the three of them in their uniforms. "What are you all up to today?" he asks.

"Training with Sala," Nadia says. "And with Elise now that she's formally here."

"As opposed to informally," Elise says.

Nadia snorts a laugh.

Nadia's father rolls his eyes. "And you Mr. Elemental? What do they have you doing today?" The dryness in his voice makes the desert seem wet.

"I'm not sure," Aidan says. "I'm going out into

Purrost Heights where the open fields are for elemental practice." Purrost Heights is a hamlet to the north end of Port Nalrang, somewhat halfway between the east and west ends of the city. It is off the edge of the cliff a good ways, some ten miles towards the desert. On the north end he knows there is a place the military uses for training and he will be going there to meet with some other elementals.

"Who will you be working with? Do you know yet?" Nadia asks.

"A pair of water elementals for safety's sake and a sand elemental."

"Do you know their names?"

"Tsuna and Hydris are the water elementals, and Therris is the sand elemental," he says.

Nadia's eyes go wide. "Hydris," she murmurs. "We last saw him that day in Umbra." Her eyes went far away for a moment. "It feels so long ago now."

"You should come by if you can and see him again."

Nadia looks at Elise who nods and answers, "If we can I would love it."

A knock on the door precedes Salter. He comes in with a tray in hand carrying several letters. Two are light-green envelopes from the witchwire office. Mr. Oswald takes the mail and hands over the green envelopes, one to Elise and the other to Aidan. They each open them and read the contents. Aidan draws in a breath.

"We're being called to Umbra again," Elise says. Nadia is reading over her shoulder. It seems they didn't feel the need to send one directly to her as she is always partnered with Elise.

"When?" Mr. Oswald asks.

"As soon as is convenient," Aidan says, reading from his message. "They are ready to launch the ship and want us to help make final checks."

"More than that, they want us to be the special guests," Elise says in surprise. "My aunt says she contacted the Conscription Authority this morning as well to request we come back to Umbra."

"That was fast," Mr. Oswald remarks. He folds his witchwire paper and looks around at them. "Would it be too much to ask to accompany you three to the launch?"

"You want to?" Nadia asks incredulously.

"It's an historic occasion. I can leave my work for a couple weeks to go witness it." It would indeed take them a week to make the trip to Umbra. But with the launch they would likely take longer.

"It'll be more than a couple weeks I think," Nadia

says.

"They've done fine without me this long. They can manage," he says, referring to how he has been accompanying the trio while they were sorting out their legal difficulties. Mr. Oswald stands up from the table and looks around. "So it's decided. I'll make the arrangements."

He abruptly leaves the dining room without another word.

The three are left in stunned silence.

After a few beats, Aidan asks, "What did you mean by 'parameters'?"

Nadia blushes a bright red.

Elise says, "We were talking about our relationship."

Immediately, Aidan says, "I apologize. I didn't mean to pry."

"After everything we've been through, I don't think either of us minds sharing our personal lives with you," Nadia says. She is referring to the nature of the magic they enacted. After that he felt a deep familiar affection for both girls that made him wonder about their bond. Magic can open doorways where none existed before.

Aidan shakes his head. "You know, every time I think we've found a way to settle down, something comes

up and we all have to leave again."

"I know what you mean."

"I just wish we could have the opportunity to catch our breath," he says.

Nadia reaches across the table and squeezes his hand. She takes Elise's next to her as well. "I want us to stick together," she says with no prelude and no inhibition. "I don't know where things are going for us, but I know we're better off together."

A pang goes through Aidan as he thinks about the friends he's left behind in Courtthostur. Part of him knows he can never go back. He can never be the person he thought he was going to be before all this started and he changed. He reaches across the table and takes Elise's free hand. The buzz of magic pulses between the three of them. He is comforted by its warm presence.

They let go of each other's hands and Elise says, "We should get ready to go."

And as one they get up and head to the front foyer. Mr. Oswald is already there waiting, donning his overcoat. The weather turned chilly overnight, an odd shift in the season. Aidan puts on his own coat, now a fireproof duster that comes to his knees and makes him look far more sophisticated than he is. The hat is customary, but he truly feels too young to look like such an adult.

Kaye drops off the girls and Mr. Oswald at the main proving grounds before heading to the outskirts of Port Nalrang to take Aidan to Purrost Heights. There, Aidan hops out of the steam carriage and heads for the lone building in the open field. He had been instructed to meet with the other elementals there. He feels odd going into a confined building when his power is the dangerous one.

"Aidan, how are you this morning?"

The person to greet him is Hydris. They had not seen each other since that fateful day. The concern on the water elementals face is touching.

Aidan puts on a wry smile. "I'm doing better," he says. "I am still adjusting but I am enjoying the work so far." He glances around the room. Tsuna and Therris remain locked in some deep conversation and don't do more than briefly wave at him. So Aidan turns his full attention to Hydris and says, "Nadia sends her best. She and Elise are hoping to come by and see you later."

The broad smile on Hydris's face says it all. "Nadia is such a lovely person," he says. "I hope she does come to visit. I don't get to see her much."

"How did you two meet?" Aidan asks, curiosity getting the better of him.

"At the Inn between Ulheapsa and Coreton."

"Do you do most of your work in Egraria?"

"No actually. I'm originally from Matraize, so I am borrowed, so to speak." He smiles at the mention of his home. "Matraize has an abundance of water elementals, as you can imagine. So no one minds me traveling around to help. You could do something similar, you know."

"What do you mean?"

"Fire elementals go wild more often than not. But you were not born a fire elemental the way Grappley was," Hydris explains. "Like me, you gained your elemental power from someone else. And you'll probably remain a controlled fire elemental your whole life because of it."

"I don't feel controlled."

Hydris shrugs. "You're more controlled than most I have met. And besides, most fire elementals wind up in the Waste or some other wild place," he continues. "Many places, Matraize for one, need the help of a fire elemental and don't really have many if any to rely upon. That's what I mean when I say you could do the same as me."

Before Aidan can answer, their main contact calls their attention. Together they start the trek outside where the four of them will do some practical work for the day.

Aidan's mind is no longer on the fire he is about to call. Instead he is thinking of the life Hydris just painted for him. His place in the world could be anything he wanted. But he couldn't help but think of the girls. He knows how bonded they are and it's obvious they love each other even if they haven't talked about it. But he knows he feels close to them as well. He knows he doesn't want to be far from them.

He steps forward to the center of the group and looks at each of the elementals around him, all with different lives than his. In that moment he makes the conscious decision to own his life, to do as each of them had done and make decisions for themselves.

Aidan just knows now that those decisions will include having the girls in his life.

Thirty-Six

Nadia feels bittersweet as they arrive in Umbra a week later. She didn't have a lot of space to analyze her feelings, but she knows she felt it nonetheless. As they arrived in Arcta, they came with much more fanfare and a much larger party than when she was last there. It's not every day a group with an elemental, an anchor witch albeit unknown, and a writer witch all accompanied by a rising political figure makes the crossing. So the military sent six soldiers with them, half of them witches as well, and had taken no arguments to the contrary.

The one good thing is that the Chulyin's offered to host the group at their house. So once again Nadia was looking at the familiar walls of Elise's home. This time they made no pretense and opted to share Elise's room.

Which is why Elise found Nadia flopped on her bed in the afternoon the day before the launch.

Elise shut the door softly and came and lay next to Nadia.

"Are they all still down there?" Nadia asks.

"They're not going anywhere anytime soon."

Nadia reaches out and takes Elise's hand. "I just needed some peace for a moment. Even I find it difficult to center myself in such a chaotic crowd."

In addition to the various military types from both Egraria and Umbra, one of the Chulyin's cousins of the royal persuasion had shown up for dinner with the usual contingent of attendees. Nadia had come upstairs to change for the now-more-formal dinner and hadn't gotten off the bed in twenty minutes.

"We should go back downstairs."

"I need to change. And so do you," Nadia says. "Do I even have anything formal enough for a royal?"

Elise laughs softly. "I think Cousin Desna wouldn't notice one way or the other." She pulls herself to a sitting position and looks down at Nadia. "Besides, you'll be beautiful no matter what you wear."

Nadia looks up at her. She is used to compliments between friends, but the intimacy of the remark got her.

She puts her hand up to Elise's cheek. Their relationship change still feels in its infancy, but somehow it also feels like they had always been this way. She sits up and nuzzles Elise's nose with her own. Then she kisses her, savoring the moment as if they wouldn't get many moments in the next few days. They probably wouldn't.

After a moment has passed and they both catch their breath, Elise says, "I can help you pick out a dress."

"I was thinking my green one."

"That would work," Elise says. "Or the red one." She waggles her eyebrows. The neckline on the red one is notoriously low and has raised more than one eyebrow.

Nadia fights a smile. "I think we should save that for the after celebration."

Elise gets up and pulls Nadia up off the bed. She kisses Nadia again and then goes to her closet to pull out her own deep blue velvet dress.

"We should reinstate our Sammday teatime while we're here," Nadia says suddenly. She is overcome with a wave of nostalgia thinking of the teashop on Arrowwood Alley. And thinking of Atley Bishop who they didn't have time to say goodbye to. Nadia wrote later to thank her and assure her they would visit.

"I do know a few teashops."

"Then it's settled."

Nadia pulls her dress from the closet and enlists Elise's help in lacing up the back. In return Nadia buttons all the difficult buttons on the velvet gown. It always felt ridiculous that women's clothes could be so impractical to women who want to dress themselves.

A knock on the door precedes a well-dressed version of Elise's mother.

"You girls look splendid," she says. "I'm glad I didn't catch you in the middle of something. We need to go down now."

"Is my hair fine for this?" Elise asks. She hadn't changed the style from lunch to now except to fix the few stray hairs.

"Add your crystal headband and loan Nadia your crystal comb. No one will notice."

With that she whisks out of the room and shuts the door behind her. Presumably she heads downstairs. With the two hair ornaments added as Elise's mother suggested, the girls follow suit.

About two hours later with the dinner concluded, Nadia finds herself oddly enough sitting between Cousin Desna and Elise in the parlor. She feels an odd sense of deja vu that she is sitting in the same seat as when she was told about her mother's death. This time her father sits opposite her and her now-girlfriend is holding her hand and resting her head on her shoulder in this more informal part of the evening.

"I understand you are an anchor witch," Desna says. He, like a few of the royal line, is a caster witch without much oomph behind his power. The royal line is mostly human with the witch gene coming from a powerful writer witch ancestor whose power continues to trickle down through the generations.

"I'm surprised you know about us," Nadia says with a glance at Aidan. The boy had been gazing into the fireplace, no doubt contemplating his own power, when Desna's statement caught his attention.

"It's true that few do, but the royal witches know," he says. "It helps to know your own people."

"I suppose that is true."

"Do you know any other anchors?" Elise asks sleepily.

"Just one, and for obvious reasons I'll decline to say who."

Perhaps he meant Wilhelm, but it might be some other anchor they don't know about.

Desna's attention turns to Aidan and he asks, "Was it

your power first?"

"Yes, and I lost it when I gained my elemental power," he said.

Desna nodded. "When I heard about our cousin here gaining a writer witch's powers, I wondered about the circumstances," he says. "It makes sense now though." His gaze goes to Nadia's father as he says, "And you know about this."

"Yes," her father answers. "But not by choice. It was necessary to represent their case with the Conscription Authority and I needed to know the facts." He shrugs. "She is my daughter and also my client. I wouldn't betray the truth."

The statement has Nadia staring at her father agape. It is perhaps the most loyal thing he has ever said about her in her life and she is utterly flummoxed.

Elise squeezes her hand. Nadia closes her mouth.

Elise's mother makes the rounds handing them all coffee for their after dinner digestif. Nadia and Elise take theirs gratefully. Elise is still falling asleep.

For a moment no one speaks while they drink their coffee. Then Mr. Chulyin asks, "What word is there about Ecrium?"

None of them had had time to pay attention to the

witchwire news lately. But Ecrium had started up again going after Rebluinia. The hiatus Nadia had bought them lasted less than a month. She felt regretful that it couldn't buy more time or end it all together. But perhaps it just proved that magic could not do what diplomacy could.

As the conversation turns to politics and Cousin Desna rises to prepare to leave, the girls set their coffee cups down and lean onto each other half-awake after all. The room briefly empties except for Nadia's father and Aidan. The four of them seem to be caught together so often these days.

"Will you two do a commitment ceremony while we're here?"

The question comes from Nadia's father and is such a shock that it completely wakes both of them up.

"We haven't talked about it," Nadia says.

A commitment ceremony is not nearly as formal as a marriage but is a way of expressing that a relationship is serious. They are too young to do a marriage anyway, but to have a small commitment ceremony is common even among teenagers.

"Perhaps you should," he continues. "It would give Elise's family the opportunity to attend, for example."

"Can I witness for you?" Aidan asks. Instead of the

traditional two witnesses of a marriage, a commitment only calls for one. And that person is usually a close friend.

Elise laces her fingers with Nadia's and answers for them both. "We would love that."

"What would you love?" Mrs. Chulyin asks upon returning to the room with her husband in tow. The last of the guests have left by now and the clock reads almost eleven.

"If Aidan would witness their commitment ceremony," Nadia's father explains. "I asked if they wanted to do one here so Elise's family could be in attendance."

Elise's mother looks at them in delighted surprise and takes her husband's hand. "I hadn't even thought of that!" she exclaims. "Are you planning on doing one?"

"We hadn't thought of it either," Nadia admits.

"But you are planning on doing one?"

Nadia doesn't need to look at Elise to know they agree. "Yes."

"Can it wait till after the launch?" Elise asks.

"I would suggest waiting till the day after if that is enough time for the both of you," Mrs. Chulyin says. "Then you could hold it in the afternoon and use the palace dinner as your celebration as well." She waves it off with a hand though and adds, "Talk it over tonight when you go up. There is no rush."

"Speaking of—," Elise says around a spectacular yawn.

"Yes, you should go to bed, all of you," Mrs. Chulyin says, including Aidan in the statement.

The three of them rise and bid goodnight to the parents. Then they make their way up the stairs, Aidan to Nadia's old room, and the girls to Elise's.

With the door shut and the sounds of their parents' voices muffled, Elise asks, "Would we be crazy to do it so soon?"

Nadia shrugs, sitting on the bed. "I think about all the time we've known each other and how many times we've gone out to tea or dinner or shopping or whatever. And I can't help but feel like we have a years-long start on this whole thing."

"Like we've been in this all along?"

"Something like that."

"Then it wouldn't be soon," Elise says. "We'd just be really late."

Nadia laughs. Elise comes to her and puts her arms around Nadia's shoulders. Nadia leans her head onto her girlfriend's stomach and hugs her waist. She feels at ease with everything.

"We should get some rest."

"And then break the news that we're going through with it."

Nadia kisses Elise's stomach, the velvet gown brushing on her lips. "I love you." The words fall out without intention. She looks up at Elise's dark eyes.

"I love you too."

And then they both are too tired for more conversation. So once again they help each other out of their intricate gowns and change into nightclothes. Before long Elise has extinguished all the lights in the room and the two are cuddled in bed together.

In her heart, the interlacing of anchor power feels totally restful and at ease. Here is where Nadia is home.

Epilogue

From a distance the ship looks almost elegant. In reality Aidan knows it is about as elegant as a boulder. The group of them had been ushered to an observation tower where they could safely watch the launch from a distance. Here, the whole launch site sprawls out before them.

The smaller test-ship would be launched today with no passengers and only the mechanical and witch programming to guide it. If the readings went well and the dummies came back unharmed, then they would be launching two passengers next month. This however is the historic first attempt.

The slingshot tower stood at a height taller than even the highest skyscraper in Cristalspire. Nothing in Port Nalrang came close to that. So, from their first-floor observatory, Aidan craned his neck back knowing he would be running outside with the rest of them when it was safe to do so. The ship would be shot into space from the launch tower with the ionic and witch power propulsion engines kicking in after that. The real test would come at the top of the atmosphere. Magic had not been tested beyond that point.

Aidan feels optimistic today.

The countdown calls out behind them through a speaker on the wall. The time is coming short. Only about ten minutes till the launch.

The ship sits at the base of the slingshot tower. The grounds around the tower have been cleared. In the far distance, Aidan knows there are some watchers on the hills he can see on the horizon. The launch would be visible from quite a distance away. The historicism of the event did not escape him.

"Are you ready?" Nadia whispers to Elise and to him.

Elise just nods. Aidan doesn't find words. He doesn't know how he feels in that moment. There is so much riding on this one launch that he is nervous for them that they'll fail. The best they can all do is wait and watch. They have all done their jobs.

Somewhere in the floors above them, Kensa is

leading the charge in the control room. The launch is her baby and Aidan knows how much this means to her. So, they continue to wait the last few minutes.

The speaker calls out, "T minus five minutes."

The slingshot lights up. Already active and ready to go, now the ship clamps are set in motion, drawing the ship to the farthest point back. There, the ship sits like an arrow drawn back on the string. Ready as ever to be thrust into space.

The minutes tick by and the callouts get closer to launch. Then the time has come. And Aidan draws a breath as the ship begins to move. It flies down the track and up the tower, shooting up into the atmosphere like a faltering bumble bee.

Beneath them the floor rumbles.

The crowd behind them begins to bustle out the back door. Aidan follows behind Nadia and Elise down the stairwell. A few minutes later they are down on the ground floor and walking out into the arid dustiness of the launching field. The three of them walk to the front of the group, their backs to the building and all the other people.

Aidan cranes his head back and peers into the sky, watching the line of cloud coming from the ship's engines.   As he watches, the light recedes into the distance, so far up and unfathomably beyond the farthest any ship had travelled before.

"Incredible," Elise whispers next to him.

In his heart the fire swells but does not go past what he chooses to hold it at. He feels the strength of the fire in the sky. He feels the pull of the element within.

He reaches out and takes Elise's hand. On her other side, she reaches out and takes Nadia's hand. The three of them stand in stark silence just watching the disappearing ship. In Aidan's heart he goes with the ship into the far reaches of space and beyond, to Yddril and to the other planets, all the way out to the last planet Laran. Maybe one day he would travel there.

Maybe one day there would be peace again on their planet. Maybe they would welcome the Yddrilin to Terra. Maybe they would move into an era of interplanetary travel.

At that moment, nothing seems beyond possibility.

At that moment, Aidan feels at peace.

Appendix

The Three Laws

<u>The Root Law</u>: Energy is the root of Magic. Magic is the root of Power.

<u>The Law of the Human Constant</u>: All species have Energy. Only humans do not have Magic.

<u>The Conservation Law</u>: All magic is conserved.

Consequences of the Laws

<u>The Witch's Constant</u>: Magic converts energy to power through the Witch's Constant.

<u>The Vacancy Principle</u>: If a witch is in contact with a human at death, the witch's magic will be conserved by the human. If no human is present, the magic will move to the witch population as a whole and be shared amongst them.

<u>The Replacement Principle</u>: An elemental's power is stronger overall than a witch's and thus will replace a witch's if released from an elemental, i.e., if an elemental dies in contact with a witch. The witch's power will also be conserved.

<u>The Rarity Conundrum</u>: The rarer a witch's power, the stronger it is and the higher in the power hierarchy it is.

Power Hierarchy

Anchor

Writer

Caster

Seer

Days of the Week

Solday

Anday

Tisday

Wodenday

Sammday

Vriday

Epday

Planet Names

	On Terra	On Yddril
Sun	Usil	Usil
1	Turms	Taira-t-il
2	Sethlans	Deyjil
3	Turan	Yddril
4	Terra	Anata-il
5	Uni	Zasil
6	Tinia	Imma-il
7	Nethuns	Oye-t-il
8/9	Aplu/Aritimi	Iedil/Avinil
10	Catha	Eiji-t-il
11	Laran	Iffta-il

ABOUT THE AUTHOR

Olivia "Lollie" Jones Black has been writing in some form or other since she was eleven. Her writing provides an emotional and creative outlet during this chaotic time. With work spanning a broad range of themes and worlds, she brings the reader to places both familiar and far away.

A background in science provides inspiration for her work. Her writing blends both science fiction and fantasy, epic and mundane.

Her previous works include *Altair*, *Linguist*, and *Plague of the Lost Ones*.

A cat who thinks she owns the computer occasionally helps with the writing. She lives on the east coast.

www.ingramcontent.com/pod-product-compliance
Lightning Source LLC
Chambersburg PA
CBHW031003190726
48285CB00004BB/1447